THE
GIRL
WITH THE
ZIPPED-UP
LIPS

BY JOHN CALLAGHAN

GW00775838

Thanks to Alex, Mabel, Julie, Jo, Jan, Adi, Martha, Lucy, Bren and anyone else who contributed in their own small way to the inking process. Huge thanks to Lisa at Lisa Lu Creations for her boundless talent and endless patience.

Follow on Instagram
@_zipped_up_lips

Book cover designed by
Lisa Lu Creations
www.etsy.com/shop/LisaLusCreations

Also available for download on Amazon Kindle

Do mo mháthair agus m'athair
and all my other teachers
who lent me theirs
and helped me find mine.

John xx

"A loud mind is greater than a loud mouth."

Matshona Dhliwayo

1

Welcome to Ickleton

Everybody dreads their *first day* at school, but by the time I turned eleven, I had already dreaded three first days in three different schools and...

DAY OF DREAD #4

...was rushing towards me faster than a blood-thirsty bulldog strapped to a rocket.

If that wasn't bad enough, the triple whammy of a new school, new house and new area left my chances of survival at a dangerously low 13%.

"This will be the fresh start we need," my optimistic father gushed before crossing his fingers and turning the key in his van-shaped rust bucket.

As the engine finally spluttered a chesty cough, I spluttered a huge sigh. I was sure my *extra* suitcase stuffed with mum's collection of hardback art books (and a couple of hidden bricks) would discourage the corroded camper from moving.

"And we'll visit mum's memorial tree whenever you wish," he assured.

I didn't reply.

I couldn't. Though we were leaving friends and taking memories, I longed to pic 'n' mix; take a few friends, leave a few memories. As we drove down Kensington Row, the shadow of the apartment block faded in the distance, and I comforted myself with the knowledge that I still had one good thing in this strange universe: my kind and patient father.

As it was me, my temper and a broken

tennis racket that had turned my last *fresh* start stale, I owed it to dad to at least give it a go.

Inner London and South Suffolk were less than a two-hour drive apart, but as a carved, wooden sign welcomed us to Ickleton, I felt so far from home and too far from mum.

Everything seemed so neat and too tidy. The entire village looked like it belonged in an episode of *Thomas the Tank Engine*. Every lawn was edged with flowers. Every hedge neatly trimmed.

Every single house was perfectly painted in soft, soothing colours with hand-crafted nameplates that read...

...*Leafy Cottage*...

...*Pippins Place*...

...*Ye Old Bakery*.

Though I hadn't yet set eyes on my new home, I had already decided to call it...

STINKIN' SCREAMIN' RUBBISH HOLE!

Searching for our new nest at No. 7, Cuckoo Hill, we drove around the *grand metropolis* of Ickleton which boasted three pubs, two churches, one post office, one school, one car garage and a tiny village hall.

While tutting in utter disgust, I also discovered that this 'village that time forgot' had ZERO cinemas, ZILCHO skate parks and the nearest KFC was almost certainly in Kentucky.

With my fourth *first day* creeping closer, I was keen to sneak a peek at my newest (and hopefully LAST EVER!) 'little' school. Despite its strange name, *Thrive Academy* was a typical, "small village" primary with one rectangular, single story building adjacent to a large assembly hall.

I prayed school #4 would (somehow) be free of the big mouths and bullies who historically inspired my fists to clench and my arms to swing. Being in Year 6 meant I had less than ten months left of my primary school sentence and more importantly, the countdown to complete *Willow Hushley's Five-Step Plan for an Ha!Mazing! Life* was tick-tick-ticking,

Step 1. Start and finish writing my debut novel, *Surfing on Starlight.*

Step 2. Email it to Bloomsbury books who will instantly publish it and stack it in every bookshop where it will sell billions (because it's Ha!Mazing!) making me millions and crowning me, W. G. Hushley, the new J. K. Rowling.

Step 3. Because I am the new J. K. Rowling (and filthy rich), I will never have to go to secondary school or sit an exam or talk to anyone ever again and I will spend all my days in STINKIN' SCREAMIN' RUBBISH HOLE writing until my fingers go numb before taking long walks in the countryside to clear my head, revive my fingers and dream up my next masterpiece.

Step 4. Spend every evening flicking through the 1.8 million pictures of scrummy-yummy cakes on #cakesofinstagram (which I will slobber and drool over but never actually bake.)

Step 5. Visit dad every Sunday in his new mansion which I bought for him (because I am filthy rich) and treat him to long, expensive lunches (because I am filthy rich).

Before any of that could happen, I had to prepare for my first day at Thrive Academy. In *0.3* seconds, I'd emptied my suitcase of the hoodies, lounge pants, sketchbooks, laptop and noise cancelling headphones stuffed inside.

"I'll sort out the TV and Wi-Fi once I get paid," dad promised while struggling to boil three eggs on the digital hob (or the "ridiculously complex puzzle that would happily see us starve!" as he called it.)

The post-boiled-egg-and-soldiers dinner entertainment was an intense, sweat-inducing wrestling match between myself, my quilt and my bed sheets (I won, but only just.) After that little tussle, I bounced downstairs and claimed my favourite new armchair. Poised with pencil, I was all set to doodle my latest butterfly design when dad marched into the lounge and lobbed a fat, black package onto my lap,

"Please try these on now and not in the morning. We need to make sure they fit," he insisted in a tired voice.

Thrive Academy's uniform was an optical abomination. Honestly, it was *EVERYTHING* a tall, skinny eleven-year-old girl could ever dream of: a storm-cloud grey blouse with a pleated, dark-navy skirt and a dull, baggy-blue cardigan. And this eye-sore ensemble just *could* not be complete without a neck-strangling, blue and grey striped tie. My reflection suggested I was about to start working as an air-hostess for **Dismal-Airlines** – not a primary school student whose main objectives for the day were surviving circle time and not wetting myself. At least my bright, orange mop livened up this costume of doom.

Despite trying every trick in the book to stay up late and delay the arrival of *DAY OF DREAD #4*, dad gave the order just after nine, "Bedtime mouse. Big day incoming! Go brush your teeth, and I'll come tuck you in."

I knew I wasn't the only one dreading their first day. Dad was surviving all the same stuff and more. My three vital responsibilities were charging my laptop, sharpening my drawing-pencils and showering while he juggled everything else. He tried so hard to be strong, but I could tell how much he missed mum by how restless he was; he could never sit in one place or stay still for more than five seconds. As he popped in to say goodnight, my jelly bean lamp was all that stood between us and darkness.

"I'll walk you down, I won't leave 'til you're in and I promise I'll be there when it ends. And ... I've already double-triple-checked that your headphones are in your bag," dad assured while scratching his greying stubble, "can this please be the last one? Don't fight them - ignore them and just walk away. We've got a big enough fight on our hands already."

He paused a moment to check if any of this information was travelling beyond my blank stare. A quick nod and a pencil-thin smile were enough to convince him that his request had reached its destination.

"I know you won't want to talk to them," he confessed as he pushed himself from the side of my bed and kissed me gently on the forehead, "but maybe try a few words – nothing more than three letters long - a 'yes' here or a 'no' there might well keep them off your back, it might even help them think you're … that you're …"

He paused and blushed as he swept all the words he shouldn't say from his tongue.

"…well, they might just think you're okay," he blurted as he rubbed his head and sighed before asking, "will you?"

99% of me wanted to scream 'YES!' there and then. A big, fat 'YES!' loud enough to scatter pigeons and startle our neighbours from their sofa cushions. But yet again, the 1% proved victorious.

Gripping my bedsheets, I pulled them up over my shoulders and turned to face the wall.

2

Ready to Thrive?

By 8.35 am, I was full of honey hoops and imprisoned inside my vile-tastic *Dismal-Air* uniform. As bad as I looked, I felt even worse. My dread levels were dangerously high. So much dread. Big dread! Colossal dread! Deep, deep dread! But at least I was dressed and dready! Sorry - ready!

Setting off on the short stroll from Cuckoo Hill to Thrive Academy, dad offered to hold my hand, but I quickly nodded no. On arriving by the royal blue school gates, my headphones helped drown out the babble of the waiting hundreds who crowded around as if someone was dishing out free cupcakes. Tongues were wagging and lips were dancing while dad and I stood on the edge of it all wishing the gates would open.

Much to my horror, everyone knew everyone. It wasn't just the parents who were yapping. All the children were clearly BFFs before they were even born. They had obviously all been delivered in the exact same hospital on the exact same day and knew all the words of all the same songs and had strange nicknames for each another like *Slurpy*, *Kipper* and *Oofy*.

I knew no-one.

Pointing at my headphones, dad motioned me to put them away, but I shook back a firm NO before pressing them further into my ears. As I did so, my second fright arrived. At precisely 8.55 am, a loud and spiteful alarm filled my ears. Every school bell I have ever encountered has been an unwelcome lug crawler, but Thrive Academy's sounded like a posse of pigs all vomiting at once, ***Bleeuurrgh-ooiinnK!*** ***Bleeuurrgh-ooiinnK!***

A cold, mechanical voice then announced,

"RANKING ASSEMBLY WILL BEGIN IN
FIVE MINUTES."

Gripping my father's hand, I stared at the ground to avoid eye contact with the strange, unfamiliar faces crowding around. Though the boar-blast briefly silenced the gang of gasbags; the motor mouths soon revved up again while Dad and I stood in silence. The timely, gentle squeeze of my hand was all he needed to say.

From out of nowhere, a most beautiful butterfly fluttered over my shoulder and landed on the back of my right hand. Its hind wings pulsed with an electric blue while a bright orange blush tipped its darker forewings. Its tiny, eyelash legs tickled my skin while holding firm against the breeze. For a moment, it was so still, it looked like a tattoo upon my hand.

"Come with me," I whispered as I drew it near.

But the moment the gate creaked open, my butterfly departed, and our fleeting friendship ended. Automatically, I followed the crowd who pushed impatiently through the gate, but after a few steps, my right arm refused to comply. Dad's left arm was anchored and staying where he stood.

"Smile and say 'hi'," he begged one final time before releasing my hand, "I promise they'll leave you alone and I'll be right here when it's over."

Trudging through the gate, my heart hammered and my soul wobbled. Of course, I knew dad would be there, but it was who wouldn't be waiting that troubled me. Many of my new school*mates* had their mums to fuss over their crumpled collars or try (for one final time) to tame that lock of unruly hair. A few students boasted the *Complete Mum & Dad Collection*, but I was the only one with just dad. I had missed her many times in many ways, but that morning, I missed her more than ever.

"RANKING WILL BEGIN IN TWO MINUTES," the toneless, robot voice boomed the instant I slipped my headphones from my ears and rested them on my shoulders. Without instruction, the waiting crowd began sorting itself into four random rows in front of the assembly hall door. Though everyone appeared to know exactly what they were doing, I was utterly bewildered because each line was a messy mix of different ages, heights and genders.

All they had in common was the puke-provoking *Dismal-Air* uniform (although I was intrigued by the small handful who sported bright, golden ties instead of the blue and grey cobra.) Keen to blend in, I did a lightning fast *eeny-meeny-miny-moe* in my head and joined the second row. At eight-fifty-nine, the heavy, wooden doors groaned open and the random lines rushed forward as if Willy Wonka was re-opening his chocolate factory.

My stomach somersaulted and pole-vaulted as an overpowering urge to retreat back through the school gate pulsed through me. But I was locked between the first and third row, and the impatient fool behind me kept trundling forward despite the fact that my feet were parked. As quickly as it sped up, the line suddenly stopped. Something was causing traffic yet my shove-shove shadow couldn't hit the brakes as yet another clumsy bump sent me stumbling into the brown-haired girl ahead.

"Oops!" she giggled with a glance, "you're more eager to get in there than I am."

I smiled my reply until a strange clicking noise suddenly swelled within my ears. The repeated rhythm of the *Click! Click! Click!* startled me into wrapping my headphones back over my ears. While they faded the clicking slightly, the final swine-squeal was too rowdy to run from,

Bleeuurrgh-ooiinnK!
Bleeuurrgh-ooiinnK!

The second boar blast at nine am hastened everyone as if God had pressed fast forward on his gigantic remote control. Permitting my shoving shadow to go ahead for fear he might kick the skin from my heels, I arrived inside the arched doorway and finally spotted the obstruction.

Four metal turnstiles lining the entrance made me briefly think I was entering Paddington Train-Station. Two-foot metal bars trundled as the bang'n'bump children stomped through the doorway. Someone must have written "NEWBIE" across my forehead with a sharpie because my "less eager" friend turned to help,

"Place your thumb on the scanner, collect your ticket and it will let you through," she advised loudly while still marching forward.

Cautiously, I pressed my thumb against the small rectangle of glass before a thin, green light scanned it. As soon as the light faded, a mini printer pushed a yellow, rectangular ticket from its mouth. Three large numbers in thick, black ink read **188**.

With all the huffing and puffing going on behind me, I had to venture onwards. After nudging through the turnstiles, I looked around for my helpful friend but she was gone. I was lost and alone amongst lines and lanes of strange faces. Gripping my yellow ticket, I drifted and wandered through the rows until I felt a tap upon my shoulder. It was her; the girl with the throbbing heel.

Pointing to her ear, she mouthed something,

"Can you hear me?" she asked as I yanked my headphones from my head. "You're slightly ahead of yourself," she giggled before pointing back towards the entrance. "If you're new, you start at the back of the hall. Look for your numbered rectangle on the floor."

Realising I was now the only student not in position, I nodded and hurried in the direction of her imprecise point. Searching for this mysterious rectangle was impossible because everyone's heavily polished leather shoes were covering the numbers.

"160!" I sighed as I finally spotted one.

"172." I was getting warm.

"180." Warmer.

"182." Smoking!

"186." Scorching!

"188!" I'm on fire!

Relieved it was empty, I plonked my feet within the black outline labelled with a massive 188 and spun to face the same direction as everyone else.

Dusty, blue curtains lining the front of the stage created a velour boundary between the nervous children around me and whatever was lurking behind. The stage was so vast, and the drapes were so grand, I half expected King-Kong to be hiding back there.

Suddenly, a loud *THWACK!* thundered across the hall. But it hadn't come from the stage; the entrance doors lurched open once more before the turnstile spun and clicked. Hundreds of heads swivelled and winced as the sunlight broke into the gloom around us.

While we blinked into the bright, an unimposing shadow shuffled towards the front row. Still fixing his tie, the boy whispered something in a heavy breath that sounded like, "Red light! Red light! Red light!" but I couldn't be sure. "Bread knife! Bread knife! Bread knife!" was also a strong possibility.

Neither made much sense.

"*Am I late?*" the speedy silhouette inquired before dropping his bag to the floor and taking the last remaining rectangle in the front row. Nobody answered. No one other than me dared looked his way. Everyone stared straight ahead.

Thunk! Thunk! Thunk!

A purposeful and heavy beat echoed from behind the curtains; sounding like someone hammering a wooden post into hard ground. The "*thunking*" continued until a whistling wind zipped through my ears as the heavy curtains whipped back. It was so quick and so fierce, it compelled me to shiver and blink. A rather strange looking creature stood upon the stage.

It wasn't King Kong.

"Good morning Thrive Academy!" came a

voice. A weird voice.

Not the big, booming voice that triggered childhood nightmares but a scratchy, croaky voice that made my earlobes want to fold inward. This raspy rattle was attached to a tall man with brown, quiffy hair, slightly greying at the sides.

"Good morning Mr Blafferty," the rows replied in unison without colour or feeling. I moved my lips noiselessly as I didn't know his name and didn't want to make a bad first impression.

Sporting a cobalt-blue, three-piece suit and a metallic grey tie, Mr Blafferty strode his long legs towards the tip of the stage. His wrists sparkled beneath the assembly hall lights due to the two large, golden letters holding the cuffs of his grey shirt together; **T** on his left wrist, **A** on his right. But the most curious element of this slick assortment was the glowing, golden cane fixed to his right hand.

What made it particularly bizarre was the fact that Mr Blafferty was, at most, in his late thirties and from where I stood, didn't appear to have a limp. But he sure loved to whizz that stick around. Pointing it. Leaning on it. It was like a super-shiny extension of his arm.

A semi-circle of ten yellow chairs waited patiently behind him – empty but expectant. Popping out from the right-hand side of the stage, a floating forearm offered a red leather clipboard which the principal promptly retrieved. After scanning his green eyes across it, he announced,

"Friday was another busy day of studying and testing, and the latest SMARP results tell me that we have a significant number of movers and shakers which means some of you are moving backwards and are now dangerously close to the exit," he croaked while pointing his cane towards the doorway.

As I stood there, trying and failing to soak it all in, I didn't have the foggiest what "188" or "SMARP results" meant. Although I now understood why some students wore golden ties,

"Can those of you in the top ten please promptly take your seats behind me once I call your name?" he requested.

"Jarvis Bonson ... Simon Gridlestone ... Esme Swirlington-Strutt ... Charles Strettingham ... Figgy Drizzlecott ... Montgomery Twist ... Benedict Uddin ... Tabitha Guild ... Sebastian Topple and Barnaby Rudge. Well done to you all."

After the smug smirkers took their seats, the crowd of stiff statues offered bogus congratulations with a slow, lifeless clap. As he arrived on stage, "Red light! Red light!" boy was grinning like a Cheshire cat - a grin that was about to be wiped from his face.

Just as he turned to lower his 'golden' posterior into the chair, Mr Blafferty swung his stick upright and prodded it into the boy's chest to create a mini yellow-brick bridge between them. The brown-haired boy gulped and stood still, confused by what was happening.

"Mr Topple. Were you not a smidge

belated in your arrival this morning?" the principal asked while towering over the boy with the inflamed face, "you know that tardiness results in an automatic five-point deduction meaning you no longer occupy ninth place. You are now, in fact ... twelfth," he confirmed after checking the notes on his clipboard.

"But my baby sister..." the sweaty boy pleaded.

Turning his back, the principal disregarded the boy's defence and lifted his baton to conduct the reshuffle.

"Number eleven – join us on stage. Topple, swap your tie with number eleven. You there, number twelve, move up one rectangle."

Poor Sebastian Topple (Red light! Red light! wasn't his actual name) was still attempting to explain his "belated arrival", but Mr Blafferty's ears were blocked to his grumbling,

"Mr. Topple! Kindly remove yourself from my stage or you will find yourself in the most horrible place imaginable," he paused for dramatic effect, making the stuttering boy wait for its precise geographic location,

"The **bottom** ten!" he spat like a pantomime villain who yearned for the silent, still rows of students to gasp in horror and shout, "Oh no, you wouldn't". But they didn't even blink. They had clearly witnessed this elaborate scene before.

"Red light! Red light! Red light!" the distressed boy spluttered while his cherry chops glowed.

Surrendering his throne, the new number twelve gingerly plodded down the steps, reluctantly trading ties with the new number ten as he passed.

"Now, as you all know," Mr Blafferty continued, "one student is no longer welcome through the doors of my academy. For three weeks running, Karl Shmuck was static - stationary – motionless! And if you are not moving forward - you are not making...?"

This time he did wait for a response. He waited quite some time because the comatose kids were resisting the hook. While I prayed that the AWOL word might somehow be CAKE, I was hardly going to shout that out.

"PROGRESS! You aren't making PROGRESS!" he seethed.

Sensing that this rambling lecture was only warming up, I tuned out of his brain-numbing bumbling. With my knees beginning to buckle, I was keen to meet my new teacher and start my first lesson, but little did I know that my first lesson had already begun.

"Well done seventy-six, you moved up seventeen places last week but one-twenty-three and one-four-seven, you are drifting. Time to pull those socks right up! Due to number one-eight-eight's enforced departure, we now welcome his replacement. One-eight-eight, please join us on stage."

It was the unexpected mention of "One-eight-eight" that suddenly unfolded my ears.

Scanning left and right, I prayed someone might whisper what I was supposed to do, but every head was parked in a forward position.

"ONE! EIGHT! EIGHT!" he repeated loudly.

Now on his tippy toes, he was craning his neck and aiming that cursed cane in my direction, "Are you with us?"

Briefly, I considered vaulting the turn-stiles to dashing home to STINKIN' SCREAMIN' RUBBISH HOLE. But I couldn't. I owed it to dad and my five-step plan to see this through. Moving through the lines, my breath hastened, and my palms flooded with a stream of sweat. The bag strapped to my back now felt heavier than a pregnant hippopotamus addicted to sugar-lumps.

"Nice of you to join us," the headmaster sarcastically sniped as I neared the foot of the stage. Heaving my unwilling legs up the stairs, every step felt like a doomed Everest expedition.

"One-eight-eight's replacement is Willow Hushley," he revealed, reciting the inky shapes from his clipboard before inquiring, "where is your number child?"

The crumpled ticket was stuck to the swamp of sweat within my fist.

"No, no, no, you silly girl," he replied as I clumsily held it out, "it's not a ticket; it's a label. Peel it off and stick it below your shoulder. Dear oh dear. Even the five-year-olds can get that right."

Only when I peered beneath the blinding stage lights, did I notice the sea of cold faces staring back. So thrown was I by their unblinking eyes, I stumbled backwards. Fumbling with the sticker, my sopping hands were shaking, and though it took less than ten seconds to unpeel, it felt like a fortnight.

"Welcome one-eight-eight," he announced while I rubbed the label beneath my left shoulder. "I spoke with your father on the phone last week. Seemed a decent sort of chap – but he basically begged me for a place at my school. He told me a big sob story which I suppose was rather clever of him and if I remember correctly, he's just started working at Pilgrims Garage which might be handy for a discount although I'm unlikely to ever need it as my BMW M-5 is only three weeks old - barely teething. I believe this is your fourth school, am I right?"

The question was so sudden and unexpected; I wasn't ready. I was still smarting over his "big sob story" comment.

"Hello?" he asked before tapping his cane on the wooden plank beneath my feet. "Am I right? This is your fourth school because you are incapable of keeping your feet and fists to yourself."

A sudden flush filled my cheeks which burned so bright, I feared the watching children might need sunscreen if they were exposed for too long.

At that precise moment, nothing would have given me more pleasure than whipping that silly stick from his hand and swinging it towards him until he danced. Of course, I didn't, I wanted to but I couldn't. (There were too many witnesses ☺) Eventually and reluctantly, I nodded in response to his question.

"Well, let me be crystal clear Miss Hushley. We do not tolerate fisticuffs here. If you even blow your nose in an aggressive manner, you will be looking for school number five! Now, in case you are unclear about the purpose of my academy, let me explain."

The stage lights blazed. Mr Gas Bag leaked. The ***Dismal Air*** army stared. And all the while, my trembling finger-taps were dripping with so much sweat, I had to secretly wipe my hands on the back of my cardigan.

"Every morning's ranking assembly sorts all my students, regardless of age or gender, in order of their academic ability. The top ten learners wear our prestigious golden tie while at the end of every term, the student with the lowest average score is expelled. All clear so far one-eight-eight?" he asked with a crumpled brow.

Though I responded with a brisk, wide-eyed nod, I was beginning to wonder if I could sneak my headphones on without him realising. It was perfectly possible; he seemed so in love with his own rules and his own grating voice that he likely wouldn't notice. "Jolly-good!" he chimed before inhaling deeply, "Upon the conclusion of this assembly, you will proceed to the study hall located behind this stage where you will spend two hours studying my three textbooks: *The Blafferty Book of Facts*, *The Blafferty Book of Numbers* and *The Blafferty Book of Grammar*."

What a trilogy!

These *books* sounded so boring, I felt they should come together in one big box-set called *The Blafferty Coma Collection*. On and on Mr Instruction Manual yakked, dimming the light in my eyes with every word he spoke.

"Once in the study hall, you must all sit in

assembly order. Each study desk is numbered so today you will sit at table one-eight-eight. Tomorrow? Who knows? You can't sink any lower!" he teased through a strangled laugh that gave me brief respite from his clawing voice.

Very brief respite.

"While in the study hall, my team of tutors – we have no teachers here – will assist you if you have questions. Just raise your hand and wait. At eleven-fifteen, you are permitted a short interval to stretch your legs and eat some fruit before returning at eleven-thirty to complete two more hours of study..."

On and on, he droned like a kitchen extractor fan,

"... you will then have fifteen minutes for lunch but you can, as many do, remain in the study hall to cram a few more facts into your skull. At one-forty-five, you will sit your SMARP Exam; one hundred and eighty-eight questions testing you on all three of my textbooks."

188 QUESTIONS!!!

15 MINUTES FOR LUNCH!!

My ears were dying. My eyes were fading. Please tell me you only do this on Mondays, I hoped. I prayed. Surely, this can't be the daily routine! What about learning to play the recorder? What about painting butterflies and writing stories about foiling bank robbers or winning singing competitions? When were we supposed to read about the adventures of Charlie and Matilda before writing poems about ice-cream and rainbows?

As Blafferty droned on, my eye-light was lower than a five-watt bulb. It was already the longest school day of my life and we hadn't even left the assembly hall.

"At three-fifteen, you feed your exam paper into my SMARP machine which stands for Super Mechanical Academic Ranking Programme and this sophisticated, state of the art technology which cost a million pounds to create will mark your paper overnight, calculate your score and rank you in position for tomorrow's assembly."

TOMORROW???

Though the words didn't tumble from my lips, my eyes were suddenly recharged and glowing like a hundred-watt bulb.

He'd noticed.

"Are you in pain one-eight-eight? Have I declared something that's distressed you?" he bluntly asked.

My eyelashes fluttered, and my breathing quickened as I promptly shook my head and shrugged my shoulders. I was sure I'd soon have to speak, that he would insist I reply with a firm, "Yes, sir!" but he didn't. He desired the sound of only one voice: his.

"Remember one-eight-eight, the sole purpose of my academy is progress! You work hard, you learn, you move up the ranks, and soon you will position yourself amongst the elite; a member of the Golden Tie Club. If you don't make progress - sob-story or no sob-story - you are out! And someone from my impressively long waiting list will take your place!"

Desperate to depart that stage, I twitched my feet a millimetre to the right, but he wasn't done with me yet.

"Are you up to the challenge 188?" he queried with a raised brow.

Because I had already nodded *YES*, *NO* and exhausted my special wide-eyed nod trick, I felt like I had to say something. If I didn't, they would all know. He stared. They all stared. The ten behind me. The one hundred and seventy-seven in front. The tall ones. The little ones. EVERYONE! After four seconds of silence, another nod would look absurd. Doing all I could think to do, the only thing that popped into my head, my last possible resort other than talking ... I saluted.

Yes, I know it was weird, but it was all I could think to do. It really could have gone either way; too quick or too animated and it might seem sarcastic and mocking; too slow and too sloppy and it might appear insincere and rude. I prayed that those watching over me might help in whatever way they could.

So, I on my first day while standing on the stage saluted the head-teacher: a big, straight-armed salute right out of nowhere. He blinked. I held my breath. By now, my sweaty fingers were spraying like super-charged water blasters. Another never-ending second ticked by before he … SMILED. Sergeant Windbag smiled and saluted back,

"Excellent one-eight-eight! I think we've found ourselves a stellar recruit!" he wheezed before pointing his cane at one boy perched upon a golden throne. "You better watch your back Bonson! She's coming for your seat!"

Breathing out a hot-air balloon sized sigh of relief, I hurried down the steps towards my numbered rectangle so fast, it was impossible not to break into a sprint. Although we had known each other for barely ten minutes, that beautiful rectangle was now my refuge, my sanctuary.

The previous night I was so, so restless

worrying about starting at school number four, but now I realised I need not have bothered because Thrive Academy was not a school. It was a prison with textbooks! Four hours of studying followed by a ninety minute, one hundred and eighty-eight question exam.

FIVE DAYS A WEEK!

"Please beam me back to my old school where my enemies can call me "Carrot Top" and "Silent Suzie" all day and I won't ever complain again," I thought as I gratefully reached rectangle #188.

Shutting my eyes, I plugged my fingers into my ears and felt a calm wave of relief wash over me.

3

Amazing Jaffa Cakes

The rest of my first day at school #4 was super-duper-dull. Though I had prepared myself for some petty name calling and evil eyeballing, by lunchtime my only fight was with the lid of my new lunchbox. (I won, but only just.)

For four endless hours, we sat in silence. Apart from the goody-goody golden gang fastened to the front row, everyone else dashed for the playground like one-hundred-metre sprinters the instant the break-time *bleurghoink* rang out. While I sucked the flavour out of a few raisins, *Mr Blafferty's Guide to Long Division* sucked the joy out of me.

Half a second before her voice arrived, I felt a small shadow loom over me,

"I think I owe you an apology," offered a

kind tone with shining, hazelnut eyes, "I should have warned you it was a sticker and not a ticket."

It was the girl who helped me defeat the turnstile that morning.

"I often mix things up" she continued, "I once mistook a banana for a mobile phone. The 4G was rubbish, but it was a perfectly delicious snack."

Expecting at least a giggle, her large, chocolate button pupils stared through me like I had three heads, but I could only smile back.

"I'm A.J. by the way" she revealed before surrendering in the impromptu game of blink. "Seeing as I know your name, I think it's only fair you know mine. I could tell you what it's short for, but it's a long story, and I think that weird pig noise is about to honk."

Right on cue, the swine-squeal, signalling the end of break time, summoned A.J. back to her table.

"Maybe see you at lunch?" she asked while

turning to walk away. My gentle nod was enough to convince her I was normal. However, the minute she turned her back, I hurriedly pulled my headphones over my ears, closed my eyes and breathed a sigh of relief.

Two more hours of studying *Blafferty's guide to this* and *Blafferty's guide to that* almost drove me loopy-bonkers-insane. I had no idea what I was supposed to be studying or how much of it or for how long. All I could do was scan through as many pages as possible and hope that questions on those topics would somehow come up. Each of Blafferty's "ingenious textbooks" was four hundred pages thick so unless I could speed-read like The Flash, I was never going to finish one book, never mind three.

Five minutes into lunch break, I felt brave enough to depart my desk in search of a toilet. Keeping my eyes fixed firmly on the ground and the random leather shoes that littered it, I weaved in and out of shouting, shuffling bodies until I spied the sacred symbol of the skirted woman. Despite sensing a few lingering looks, everyone seemed too absorbed in their quest to enjoy their brief lunchtime freedom to bother with the new girl.

As I exited the loo, I immediately spotted A.J.'s frizzy brown curls at the top of the corridor. Three students were crowding around her, and although I could only see the back of their heads, the startled look in her eyes communicated her discomfort. Edging towards them, I pushed my headphones from my ears and listened in.

"I see A.J.'s got a new friend!" a boy with floppy blond hair sniped in a nasty tone while the boy and girl either side of him agreed with grunts and giggles.

"Yeah, she's nice." A.J. replied meekly before trying to push past but they quickly closed shoulders to bar her way.

"Blafferty said her name's Willow, but we still have no idea what A.J. stands for?" he jeered.

Now only a few feet behind, A.J. spotted me but this wasn't the bright and breezy girl that joked about her banana phone at break-time. She was blinking and jittery while her body was shrunken.

"Does it stand for Awesome Jellyfish?" the blonde boy asked, stirring a chortle from his sidekicks.

"I think it's Amazing Jaffa Cakes!" the tall boy on the right with short, dark hair suggested.

In an attempt to play along, A.J. squeezed out a small laugh.

"What about Absolute Joke?" the girl on the left with the tight, blonde ponytail proposed.

I was now swinging distance from the back of their heads. My fists were poised and clenched. All I needed was the green-light from A.J., but her eyes were flashing red.

Their next *guess* left me needing no invitation,

"You're all wrong. I've got it," the middle boy advised, "A.J. stands for... African Jungle."

I lunged for the back of his shiny, blonde head but as soon as I did, A.J. jumped between us and pushed me back so forcefully, we both fell to the floor.

"What the?" the bullies spluttered amidst the confusion before sprinting down the corridor, cackling like hyenas.

"No need to start school number five on my account!" A.J. said as she reached out a hand to heave me upright.

I wanted to tell her the million different ways she should get revenge but I couldn't so I just stared at her until she felt so awkward, she retreated into the girl's toilets. I was so incensed by what I had just witnessed, but I didn't know what to do. I wandered around trying to find Mr Blafferty's office so I could somehow enlighten him about what was going on in his school. Despite discovering a fancy, wooden door with his name spelt out in thick, golden letters across the top, it was locked.

Wandering back towards the study hall, I

was startled to find A.J. waiting by my desk. With a completely straight face, she held a large, yellow banana to her ear,

"I'll have seven of the sleeveless dresses in burgundy and make sure those turtle doves are actually still alive when they get here! You know what happened last time Donna!" she demanded with mock aggression before slamming her fruit-phone down upon the table. "Honestly! Why I bother paying these people a wage, I just don't know!"

Though a giggle gurgled up my throat, I had to resist it. As I walked around her to get to my desk, she made a rather shocking revelation.

"I think we're related," she proclaimed with a straight face as I settled into my grey plastic chair. My frown was enough of a cue for her to proceed.

"Ickleton is a tiny village and that boy that you saw losing his tie today, the "red light, red light" boy. Well, his name's Sebastian Topple, and my dad's sister is his mum which makes him my cousin even though he's white and I'm ... not," she explained while moving her fingers through the air, trying to connect the branches on this strange, invisible family tree.

"And his dad, Gerald, who's married to my dad's sister is the co-owner of Pilgrims Garage which is where your dad works, so we're related."

Other than throwing my hands in the air with a shrug, I couldn't think of any other way to communicate how bonkers and bizarre this family tie was.

"I know because you're white and I'm not that you probably think it's weird but it is possible you know," she clarified.

I could feel the long story that she'd previewed earlier was about to hit the big screen,

"My dad met my mum when he was travelling around Zimbabwe, and she moved back to live with him here. I've never been, but mum says we're definitely going before I start secondary school. I would so love to meet my grandparents and see what mum's life was like when she was little. Anyway, I'm talking too much. Where did you move from?"

It was her first inescapable question; a question I couldn't nod away. I had already begun to tune out of her rambling but now I had to do something. A stupid salute wasn't going to save me this time.

"Have I gone deaf or do you not talk?'" she asked while pulling up the chair from the desk in front and sliding it alongside mine before she began unpeeling her bruised banana phone.

"It's okay if you don't or ... can't?"

Her head twisted slightly to the side as she lingered a moment. Sensing my unwillingness to respond, she proceeded,

"I've never met someone who didn't talk but you've probably never met someone who's half Zimbabwean, so let's call it even. Because I don't look enough like them, nobody really talks to me and you don't seem to want to talk so if it's okay – I'll just talk to you but, don't freak out, I won't burn your ears off or anything."

With that, she stood up and slid the chair back into position while I tried to suppress the enormous sigh of relief bumbling behind my lips. She certainly could talk.

"Anyway, thank you for what you did earlier with Jarvis, Simon and Figgy but trust me, they're members of the golden tie club which means Blafferty won't do anything. And because their parents are all governors, they think they run the school which is flutterly fantabulous. Anyhow, it's only words, they've never hit me."

There was so much I wanted to say. So many of her words were wrong and I wanted to put them right, but I couldn't risk it.

I was too afraid.

"Good luck in your first exam and if you want a tiny tip from me: just answer enough questions to stay in the middle. I only answer the ones I'm definitely sure of. Seventy definites puts me between rectangles ninety and a hundred which keeps me hidden in the middle and stops him from ever talking to me. It works for me but hey, it's up to you. Being the only black girl gets me enough attention already."

As she strolled back to her desk, the boar blast signalling the end of lunch sucked everyone in from the playground before Blafferty could grumble about their "belated arrival".

Taking A.J.'s advice, I only answered the 'definites'. Some questions were really easy and clearly designed for the younger students, but I soon realised just how smart the top ten really were.

The final fifty questions were super-duper tough, hard as concrete. Once I hit seventy definites, I scribbled butterfly patterns on the question paper and watched the clock reluctantly tick,

tick,

tick towards three fifteen.

Mr Blafferty claimed SMARP education would take learning to a new level, but the only new levels I was feeling were NEW SKY-SCRAPER HIGH LEVELS OF BOREDOM WITH SUPER-SIZED YAWNS WIDE ENOUGH TO CRACK MY JAW OPEN!

After the longest day in the history of days and time and clocks and forever, Mr Blafferty folded up his noisy newspaper and rose from his desk,

"Pens and pencils down people. Your first SMARP exam of the week is complete."

Being number 188 meant I was last to feed my exam paper into his weird mechanical thingy. This "super" SMARP machine looked like something that belonged in the school's boiler room.

As tall as a wheelie-bin and as wide as a garage door, this shiny metal box grew out of the back wall of the study hall, just to the right of Mr Blafferty's desk. Thick translucent tubes sprouted from all sides like digital dreadlocks. The second I fed my exam into its narrow, letter-box mouth, a winding, grinding noise rumbled around inside while the tangle of tubes lit up with pulsing blue lights, giving the impression that the machine was alive and busy grading my paper.

"First one done one-eight-eight," Blafferty summarised as I turned to exit the hall. "Let's hope for a reasonable score in tomorrow's ranking assembly. It would be a shame to disappoint your father."

While, of course, I never replied, if my *charming* principal had heard just a handful of the colourful adjectives bouncing around my head, it would have most certainly been my last SMARP exam.

True to his word, dad was waiting by the gate. Running straight into his arms, I buried my head into his soft, round belly and squeezed him until his gut was a little less flabby.

"You survived!" he exclaimed before planting a kiss on the top of my head.

"How was it?" he asked, easing my head back slightly from his stomach.

"Oh," he said, spotting the tiny tears welling in the corner of each eye.

4

Mum's Lullaby

During my first seven years on earth, nothing or no-one could keep me quiet.

If I wasn't howling for a warm bottle of milk, I was in fits of giggles with Iggle Piggle.

When I wasn't singing *I'm a Little Tea-Pot*, I was peppering mum and dad with billions of questions like,

"Do spiders fart?" and "Why don't crabs have eyebrows?"

According to mum, even sleep couldn't silence me, "Do you realise you spent half the night talking to some invisible person about turning into a butterfly?" my jaded looking mother revealed one morning during breakfast.

"No, I didn't!" I bickered back.

"Yes, you did! I have proof. Look! I recorded you," she revealed in a triumphant tone.

As mum held her phone screen towards me, my porridgy fingers pressed play and there I was, rambling away while fast asleep,

"I'm tired of being a caterpillar ... it's so dull, dull, dull ... my wings will be the most beautiful in all the kingdom ... orange and blue and purple and green... and I'll never get tired of flying up and down and all around ... fly, fly, fly."

Then the silence came.

Three days after my seventh birthday, mum died. One day after that, I stopped talking. It wasn't because I was sad or angry although I experienced an immeasurable amount of both. It was her song that started my silence.

I'll never forget the moment that dad sat me down on the couch beside him. Holding my hands in his, he cleared his throat and said, "Mummy's gone to sleep Willow ... and when she wakes up ... she's going to be with Nana Rosie in heaven."

"Will Frodo be there too?" I asked, referring to my pet hamster who escaped his cage before chewing through dad's iPad charger a few months earlier.

Though I showered him with a zillion inquiries, he returned each one with patience, kindness and just a sprinkle of little, white lies. By evening, our house was wedged with visitors who dropped by to shake my hand and tell me how "sorry" they were about "losing mum". Confused by their apologies, I preferred to pass the time pouring milk and stirring sugar into the one million cups of tea that my Grandma Pat (dad's mum), my aunties and all the sympathisers were guzzling while they shared their favourite memories of mum. Dad wasn't drinking tea. He needed something stronger.

When he tucked me into bed that night, I gave him the squeeziest hug in the history of hugs and said, "I bet mum's having breakfast with Nana Rosie right now."

I figured heaven was so far away that the

clocks must be at least eight hours ahead. After he left, I turned off my jelly bean lamp and lay there in the dark trying to listen in to the storytelling that continued below. Other than the odd word, I couldn't really hear much, and it wasn't only the floorboards blocking the signal. Something else was humming through me, murmuring in my ear and the more I tuned into it, the louder it became.

It was mum.

Her soft, angelic voice flooded my ears with the same eight-line lullaby she sang to me every night until the sandman came calling. Her song spiralled through my ear so loudly, it felt like she was sitting right by my bed.

Wondering and hoping that she might somehow be in my room, my shivering fingers fumbled around my lamp, but as the small flush of light thawed the darkness, my heart sank. The room was emptier than ever. Though it had been a long and exhausting day, the anchor on the Titanic couldn't have pulled my eyelids shut.

Shuffling upright in my bed, I pinched the skin on the back of my hand to check I wasn't dreaming.

Mum's melody remained.

All night, she sang. All night, I listened, and as morning's sunrise illuminated the edges of my curtains, the songbird was still chirping. Despite my stomach's gurgling demand for a big bowl of honey hoops, I wasn't ready for the show to end.

"What if it's a one-time thing?" I worried. "What if I hear a song on the radio and it gets stuck in my head and I lose mum's lullaby?"

After a few more hours of lazing and listening, my greedy tummy was so rowdy I had to feed it. As I scuffled my slippered feet through the kitchen door, I discovered dad sitting at the kitchen table, staring into his half-drunk morning coffee.

"Morning mouse," he said in a tired, colourless tone.

"Mum sang to me all night," I revealed

while reaching for the big yellow box in the larder.

"Did she?" he asked through a crumpled brow.

"She sang her lullaby over and over and it was so loud and so clear, I thought she was in my room," I rambled while soaking my hoops with a messy splash of milk.

Rather than reply, dad plugged his lips with a long swig of coffee.

"Did mum ever record herself singing?" I inquired.

His grouchy frown suddenly coughed out an unexpected chuckle.

"Bless the heavens I still have you Willow," he laughed with a little wobble in his throat. "Your mum? Record herself singing? She wouldn't sing in the shower for fear the shampoo bottles might hear her."

"But she sang to me!" I contended.

"You were her audience of one. She reserved that V.I.P. seat in the front row just for you," he explained.

With my stomach silenced and my query answered, I darted upstairs to get dressed. Before fussing over what I should wear, I covered my ears with my hands in the hope of tuning into Radio Lullaby.

Her voice was gone.

The harder I pressed my palms against my head, the louder the silence grew. All I could hear was the echo of dad's laughter and him joking about shampoo bottles and V.I.P. seats. Suddenly a booming, growling voice invaded my ears and it definitely wasn't mum. It was loud. It was angry, and it was shouting about some sort of highway to hell. Panic ripped through me as the beat of the drums and the twang of the guitar jammed my ears. Vaulting downstairs, I stormed into the kitchen, snatched the radio from the countertop and smashed it against the hard, tile floor.

"What the?" dad barked as he jolted to his feet, spilling his coffee across the table.

"I can't hear her!" I screamed, "I can't hear her!"

After racing back to my room, I pulled my curtains shut, flounced into my bed and wrapped my quilt around me in an attempt to revive mum's voice. The thundering *thud-dum* of my heart was just beginning to calm when dad came to check on me,

"Are you all right mouse?" he whispered into the dusky room.

"Go away!" I screamed, "I NEED SILENCE!"

After waiting then trying; trying then waiting, I eventually drifted off to sleep. When I awoke a few hours later, I was relieved to find mum's soft voice floating within my ears once more. From that moment on, every time anyone made eye contact with me, I felt so scared that I might get trapped in a long conversation and lose her that I did whatever I could, no matter how strange or how rude, to shut down the dialogue.

To make sure mum never fell silent, I did.

Dad never replaced the smashed kitchen radio, and he was no longer *permitted* to play music in the car.

It took him a little while to get used to it, but no matter how frustrated he became, I couldn't let my small, blunt tongue break the seal.

In the early days, I communicated via hand-written messages in my butterfly notebook but when that got on his nerves, he bought me a mobile phone so I could text him.

With dad being a man of few words, we soon adjusted. He even asked his friend Larry, an air-traffic controller at Gatwick airport, if we could borrow a pair of noise-cancelling headphones to see if they'd help.

They were so fab, and I used them so much, I never returned them (sorry Larry!) Because they were blue, dad (in an attempt to be thoughtful) spray-painted them electric pink with a leftover can from the garage. The new colour made me want to vom so much that I had to scratch as much of the nasty, pink paint off as possible, making them a tragic mix of the original blue with faded splashes of pink; kind of like a smurf had a baby with a flamingo. Ever since, my mum's soothing lullaby has sung me to sleep because my lips have remained tightly zipped.

Well, they were until Mr Blafferty unexpectedly disappeared.

5

Mrs May...who?

Four months of school days passed by slower than a snail towing a trailer of army tanks.

Thanks to A.J.'s advice, I rose to the middle numbers and then hid there. Though it physically hurt me to do so, I answered just enough 'definites' to stay in the top hundred and wrongly answered the questions that could have pushed me towards the top ten.

34. What is the capital of Switzerland?

Every week this question came up, and without fail, I wrote *Geneva* despite being three thousand percent sure it was *Zurich*.

78. Explain the meaning of the word "specific."

This one came up every two weeks, and

although it should have been easy-peasy, I always chuckled a little after incorrectly scribbling, "It's a *mahoosive* ocean between America and China."

145. What is the square root of 196?

Every day there was a square root question that I could have easily figured out; the answer should have been 14, but I wrote 11.34 ½ or whatever random number that popped into my head.

The only question that truly needed an answer was; how was getting the same questions wrong day after day, without ever finding out the actual answer, supposed to be the future of education? During those slug-slow months, the top ten never budged.

Not once.

Every member of the golden gang sat snug on that stage, smug as emperors, sneering down at the rest of us. Despite his best efforts to regain his beloved golden tie, Sebastian Topple only travelled in one direction: south.

Week by week, he slipped further and faster down the charts and by February, he was loitering outside the top fifty. The Kings and Queens of Rumour-Ville spread 'fake' news far and wide that Sebastian's father, a parent governor, demanded to meet Mr Blafferty in order to understand why his son wasn't making the "super" progress originally promised.

According to unconfirmed reports, Mr Topple insisted on seeing the marked exam papers with his own eyes because he could not believe that fifty students were brighter than his son, particularly when Sebastian was older and smarter than most. The Gossip King, Bradley Bogstein, claimed he over-heard Mr Topple arguing with Mr Blafferty in his office,

"Seb's dad kept shouting, FIFTEEN TIMES! FIFTEEN TIMES! FIFTEEN TIMES you promised to send me those exam papers so where are they?"

The gang of wide-eared gossip hounds semi-circling Bradley demanded to know, "What did he say? What did he say?"

"I didn't catch his reply. All I know is that Mr Topple was fuming because he stormed out of the office warning Blafferty that the matter was far from over."

"Oooh!" replied the chatter monkeys while Bradley glinted under the light of the attention he craved.

Determined to avoid situations where I might yank hair or raise bruises, I dropped anchor in the study hall during break and lunchtime. Apart from the odd visit to the toilet or a visit from the odd A.J. (who never failed to brighten my day) it was easy to hibernate for hours between the pages of Blafferty's textbooks, blinking at his ink-stained *wisdom*.

After the first few days, I felt confident enough to walk home and let myself in to **STINKIN' SCREAMIN' RUBBISH HOLE!** Every day dad would arrive home a few minutes after five and ask how my day was and every day I'd text him one simple word that summed up all of my school days at Thrive Academy; "Fine."

Well, not *all* my days.

One Monday in March, something extraordinary happened. After four months, I should have no longer feared the ear-churning pig alarm and gut-twisting countdown but as I braced myself outside the school gate, neither arrived.

A mysterious silence fell upon the playground. It was so quiet I thought I'd discovered a new SUPER-SOUNDLESS mode on my head-phones. Glancing from face to face, I tried to read the situation, but all anyone could offer was a shrug. Alarmed by this unexpected change in routine, Sebastian started to fret.

"Red light! Red light!" the poor boy wailed, swaying from side to side, tapping the face of his smartwatch.

"Don't worry Seb," A.J. whispered, "he's probably just a smidge belated in his arrival."

"No! He's never late. Not even a smidge.

Red light! Red light!" he droned on, unaffected by A.J.'s kind attempt to calm his jangled nerves.

"I feel a day off coming on!" Bradley optimistically predicted.

Before anyone could even start dreaming of hours of staring at screens of different sizes, the doors of the assembly hall creaked open.

Nobody moved. Everybody glared. Briefly, I feared some wild, vicious creature might bound from the darkness to devour us all but thankfully the only thing running wild was my imagination.

While everyone continued to look to one another for some clue about what they should do, Sebastian was determined to be punctual.

Happy to follow his lead, we slunk in behind him but the instant his eyes wandered through the door, he let out a deafening shriek.

"Red light! Red light!" he cried.

"The turnstiles? THEY'RE GONE!" he sobbed.

"The finger scanners? THEY'RE GONE!" he wailed.

"The mini printers? THEY'RE GONE TOO!" he bawled.

Yet the most shocking alteration to the SMARP assembly hall was something else entirely,

CHAIRS!

One hundred and eighty-eight blue chairs (I'm a really fast counter!) were laid out in perfectly neat rows.

"Are there numbers on them?" wondered an anxious whisper nearby.

We shrugged.

We stared.

We shrugged some more until a voice, stemming from the stage, summoned a hoard of heads to swivel its way.

"Students, please sit down." the voice calmly pronounced.

It was Mr Wingman, one of Blafferty's most trusted tutors. With a sudden rush, everybody quickly pushed along the rows, knee-nudging the plastic chairs which squeaked against the hard, varnished floor.

"What's happening?" A.J. wondered while following me close behind. "Where's Blafferty?"

Within seconds, everyone was sitting, fixed and giddy, ravenous for the delivery of this fat slice of mouth-watering news. Some members of the golden gang weren't quite so thrilled about this new menu and were particularly offended by the fact that their pole position at the front of the hall had not been "reserved".

"Get up you little runt! I should be sitting there," Jarvis angrily insisted.

"I don't see your name on it?" little Timmy Weismark bravely countered.

"Please sit down Mr Bonson," Mr Wingman firmly suggested. "The governors have requested that I…" he paused to clear his throat, "…inform you that Mr Blafferty is taking an extended period of leave. As a consequence, a new, temporary head-teacher will lead daily operations within the academy until his return. Please assure your parents that we will be writing to them to explain the situation."

My head was spinning. For eleven years, I'd wished on a million shooting stars and a billion birthday candles, and finally, one of them had come true.

A break from Blafferty.

A rest from his rambling.

A change from his chattering.

At least one whole day off from his wretched ranking.

"So I would like to introduce you all to your new, temporary head-teacher - Mrs Mayhew."

Three people clapped. No one dared move. I was so excited; I could hardly breathe. As we waited - all anticipating a glimpse of our new head-teacher - nothing or no-one arrived.

"I'll go see where she's got to," Mr. Wingman blushed before scarpering off the side of the stage.

Everyone was shuffling left and right, desperate to ensure that some cannonball head or giraffe-neck wasn't going to obscure their first peek of our new principal.

"I expect a full itinerary for the day ahead," moaned Seb who sat in the row in front, massaging his temples.

"I hope..." A.J. added until four heads suddenly swivelled around to learn of her expectations. Startled by the attention, she quickly zipped her lips shut.

As the pitter-patter of tiny footsteps tickled our ears, a palpable hush enveloped everyone.

"She's here!" A.J. whispered loudly while patting my left shoulder.

There she stood: a little woman with a biscuit-brown bob. My eyes sipped her in. The green ribbon laces on her tawny shoes, the white pleated skirt dotted with green and orange flowers, her white blouse dotted with bright emerald buttons, her funky, lime-green glasses. One hundred and eighty-eight ogling observers followed her trail as she walked towards the edge of the stage.

Lowering her bottom lip, which was ever so lightly lip-sticked with a soft, rosy pink, she pushed a tiny noise from her mouth. Though fragile, this dulcet delight somehow echoed through the assembly hall. It filled every particle, every space as she, to our utter bemusement, slowly started to sing,

> *"May you always live your life,*
> *may you never find it dull.*
> *May you always love your life,*
> *may you live it to the full."*

Suddenly, she stopped. Nobody clapped. She did not bow or nod or smile or say thanks. She just stood there. Staring. My heart pounded and my pulses throbbed as a panic woke within me. Mrs Mayhew may have stopped singing, but in the lingering silence, her four-line song was swimming through me. It was dangerously hummable and wickedly memorable. Half-tempted to run from the hall, I paddled towards the edge of my seat.

"She is going to sing again," I fretted

silently while glancing around, searching for the nearest and most discrete exit. Whether I dived left or dived right, it didn't matter because I was submerged in the middle of the row, surrounded by a sea of flummoxed faces. Just as I moved to stand up, Mrs Mayhew caught my eye and shot her left hand into the air.

Right on cue, something small, grey and furry scuttled across the stage.

It was a meerkat.

Yes! A meerkat! A meerkat sporting a black top hat and bow-tie. (I swear. I don't tell lies!) As if it was the most natural thing to do, Mrs Mayhew leaned down towards this strange stage dweller, patted it on the head and handed it a tiny stick no bigger than a candy cane.

"No way I'm missing this!" I thought while sliding into the back of my chair.

Agape and aghast, we all sat in stunned silence. Well almost everyone. Bradley, sitting two rows in front, loudly announced, "That's so fake! It's obviously remote control!"

Ignoring the disbelieving heckler, the meerkat held his pee-wee pointer outwards, gripping it tightly with both hands like he was holding the handlebars of an invisible bicycle. Bradley wriggled around in his seat trying to get the best possible angle to spot the wires or mechanisms that would prove his latest conspiracy theory. He was sure that if he could stretch his neck far enough to the right, he would spy Mr Wingman expertly guiding every movement and blink of this hairy, little android with a remote control. However, Mr Wingman was nowhere to be seen, and Bradley's eyes rocketed from their sockets with what happened next.

A tat-a-tat-tat!

Mrs Mayhew did a quick five-step tap dance before suddenly stopping. I was still trying to process the fact that my head teacher was singing and dancing rather than obsessively ranking when the meerkat also started to dance. (I swear! No lie!)

A tat-a-tat-tat!

The same five steps arrived with perfect precision before the meerkat hastily halted. Wearing black and white blotch shoes no bigger than a fairy's thumb, the silver-furred creature stood side by side with Mrs Mayhew. Although not particularly tall herself, she dwarfed this cute cousin of a mongoose. Like a watchman on morning patrol, he stood there, scanning the crowd, waiting for his moment.

Pat-too-tat, Pat-too-tat!

A cool drum beat breezed through the sound system.

Pat-toot-tat, Pat-too-tat!

Just like Mr Bojangles himself, this Kalahari kicker scuffed, stamped and stomped.

As if under a spell, his pippin paws flapped and slapped a storm of breath-taking beats into the wooden planks of the assembly hall stage. So insane and so rapid was the tapping that a bunch of us mistakenly believed it had started raining outside. Tinchy black and white shoes spun and whirred like out of control lawnmower blades that built and constructed the most marvellous of beats which vibrated through the watching crowd. Shoulders instinctively shuffled as feet impulsively went *pat, pat, pat* on the old varnished floor beneath. For months, A.J. and I were happy to stay hidden in the middle, but now we both craved a seat in the front row so we could gobble up every last crumb of this scrumptious hijinks.

The mesmerising meerkat swung his cane around with such breezy charm; you would have sworn it was an extension of his arm. Disobeying gravity, this pocket-sized marvel suddenly jumped on to his tip-toes, pushed his furry knees forward and with a wave of his hand, summoned Mrs Mayhew to follow his lead. In tandem, they danced as one.

He flicked out a forward stomp.

She flicked out a forward stomp.

He scuffled a leg back.

She scuffled a leg back.

Swanky synchronicity.

Every time these dithering dancers swung or kicked their steel capped toes out into the air, sparkles of silver flashed before our eyes. These perfect performers were so cool and so unruffled, they must have practised for months.

A right leg forward ...

TIP! TAP! TIP!

A jump to the right...

TAP! TIP! TAP!

A quick step back...

Pa-Tat-Tat-Tat!

As she jiggled and wiggled her crazy feet, the green ribbons on her shoes flapped like wind-blown butterflies. It was unlike anything I had ever witnessed. This riveting paradiddle was so grin-inducing, my face began to ache.

Not everyone was so amused. Bradley was rolling his eyes while a handful of other grunt-bags tutted and folded their arms. But Mrs Mayhew and her fuzzy friend didn't seem to care as her green skirt whirled across the stage like a pushed-up umbrella. Even the perma-grump, Mr Benjamin, was spotted bopping his right foot in time to the music before he suddenly remembered himself and hastily reverted to his usual state of rigour-mortis.

Ta – toot, ta –toot, da da da ta-toot!

The rollicking repertoire of razzmatazz rolled on as these dazzling dancers worked their way back and forth, swinging their arms, shaking their open palms, smiling the most infectious smiles. This blizzard of beats and bangs, this tirade of tips and taps magnetically drew me towards the stage like they were performing for me alone.

"I don't ever want it to end," A.J. gushed in a rushed whisper.

On they tapped and on they bopped until one final, ferocious flurry. Their frantic feet flickered so fast, I was sure they were about to disconnect from their ankles and soar straight over our heads. One final **_pat-too-tat, pat-_**

too-tat, pat-too-tat-tat-tat brought the most utterly bizarre dance to a close.

I longed to clap. I longed to stand up and scream. I wanted to, but nobody else moved because nobody knew how to react; assemblies were not supposed to be like that. Lines of permanently arched eyebrows and stiff, scary smiles looked towards one another, wondering what to do. Our eyes had never been allowed near a banquet as bonkers as this. It was perfectly possible that over the course of that performance, our gaping mouths consumed at least twenty-three bugs and flies.

As Mrs Mayhew rapidly raised her right hand into the air, the tap-dancing meerkat promptly scuttled off into the shadows. Our substitute principal then stepped to the tip of the stage to sing once more,

> *"May you always live your life,*
> *may you never find it dull.*
> *May you always love your life,*
> *may you live it to the full."*

Above everyone's heads, the strained silence sagged until Mr Wingman returned to the stage and stood beside Mrs Mayhew. Retrieving a post-it from his pocket, he smoothed it out and feebly announced,

"Mrs Mayhew has decided that for the foreseeable future, you will all be taught in year groups."

Though Mr Wingman certainly had more to say, nobody could hear him due to the puzzling jumble of frenzied cheering and moo-like booing which suddenly filled the hall. Even though it was a roughly sixty-forty split in favour of the change, I was startled by the scale of the hissing herd.

"We want study hall!"

"We want study hall!"

A rowdy group of twenty or thirty near the front chanted while Mrs Mayhew looked on, slightly embarrassed.

"Quiet please!" Mr Wingman cried, trying to dampen the rebellion but his weak attempt only fanned the flames. A feisty war of words made the assembly hall seem more like the House of Commons,

"We don't like change!"

"We don't like textbooks!"

"We don't like change!"

"We don't like textbooks!"

Eventually, the sensible students united to SHUSH!!! the rowdy dissenters into a grumbling hush.

"Thank you, children. Your teachers will now lead you to your classrooms where you will spend the day exploring the world of dance."

"BOOOOOOOO!" the moaning cattle rumbled once more while we slowly filed out of the hall.

"How is dancing going to help me get into the boy's grammar?" Monty Twist snarled at no one in particular.

"I'm supposed to become a pilot. Anyone ever heard of a tap-dancing pilot?" Jarvis Bonson seethed in reply.

"I hope you saw what I saw," A.J. mumbled as she led me from the hall, "because, if you didn't, I have to stop putting sugar on my coco-pops."

6

Day of Dance

The forever plump and pink skinned Mrs Murphy was assigned "temporary" teaching duties for Year Six.

Her cheeks glowed with a feverish red beneath a broad smile as myself and umpteen other ten and eleven-year-olds filed into her classroom. Finding themselves in an ample space with no chairs, Monty Twist and Tabitha Guild immediately inspected the floor in search of a numbered rectangle. No matter how pointless and hollow a routine might be, some people just can't live without one.

"Please, sit down children, anywhere on the floor. The room's a little messy because it's been empty for so long but while you dance, I shall dust!" our new teacher assured.

"While I don't know many names, I promise I will get to know you all flickety-quick." After releasing a nervous chuckle, she offered a little flavour of what we might expect, "Today, Mrs Mayhew would like you all to experience traditional dances from around the world. You'll learn about the origins of each dance before trying on the traditional dresses and costumes. Most importantly, you will all get the opportunity to try the dance itself. Your first workshop will focus on Native American Grass Dancing, and because I can't even shuffle without three gin and tonics inside me, I will put you in the capable hands of Halana and Yazzie."

The two strangers, lurking within the frame of the door, finally entered with big smiles and little waves. The moment she spotted them, A.J. turned towards me and unleashed a grin so grand, she'd probably require a license to keep it.

"I know they don't look like me," she wheezed, "but they don't look like you either!"

"Good morning everyone," the young woman with dark chocolate hair and black-rimmed glasses offered with a smile.

"My name is Halana. This is my brother Yazzie, and we are both natives of a small town called Petoskey which you'll find in the state of Michigan in America. Our ancestors belonged to the Odawa Tribe, and today we'd like to tell you all about Grass dancing or Pow Wow dancing as it's more commonly known."

Halana and Yazzie then moved to the left of the whiteboard while Mrs Murphy played a short YouTube clip of Native American men and women dancing in a field. Their dance was so passionate, and their outfits were so vibrant, I was instantly spellbound but some of the "Neverland" boys, who refused to grow up, just had to snicker and tut.

"That's not normal!" Jarvis Bonson decreed quietly enough to be heard by everyone except Mrs Murphy and our guests. Though A.J. looked away, pretending not to have heard,

Sebastian wasn't prepared to let it go.

"You're not normal Jarvis!" he scolded in a raspy whisper, immediately drawing a flock of hostile eyes upon him.

"What's it to you? You're not Indian!" Jarvis countered, causing those behind him to fall about laughing. Finally, spotting the niggling, Mrs Murphy threw out a tame ***SSSHHHH!***

But Sebastian wouldn't be hushed,

"Indians are found in Asia. Our visitors are Native Americans. Tonight, while revising your map of the world, I suggest you also think about the fact that there is no such thing as normal because everyone's normal is different!"

By now, Mrs Murphy felt obliged to intervene.

"Excuse me, young man. I just asked you to be quiet. Please step outside and take a minute to think about why you're here!"

A.J. offered Sebastian a grateful smile but as he stood up to walk through the sitting crowd, Jarvis (the chief lost boy) sneakily grabbed his foot which sent him tumbling into the mess of heads and knees below him. Jarvis grinned and high fived Simon Gridlestone while I burned holes in the back of their heads with a vengeful stare.

After the video finished, Seb re-entered on condition of an apology to our guests and no repeated 'whispering offences'. As he returned to the floor beside me, Halana pulled her long, coffee coloured curls behind her ears and asked,

"Does anyone know who created the Pow-Wow dance?"

"Was it Justin Bieber?" Figgy Drizzlecott proposed with a straight face while everyone around her fell about laughing. She may have been one of Blafferty's golden girls, but poor old Figgy hadn't yet read *The Big Book of Common Sense*.

"Not quite," Yazzie interjected in a kind voice, "it was a little before the age of Bieber. You see, the story goes that in a time where all good stories start - long, long ago, there lived a boy called Hatoto."

Thanks to Yazzie's big voice and broad shoulders, the giggling gang managed to find enough inner peace to remain quiet.

"Like you, Hatoto was ten years old, but unlike you, he couldn't walk. Since birth, he had no power in his legs, and he relied on his mother and father to carry him everywhere. However, as Hatoto grew bigger and his parents got older, it became too difficult to carry him to where he needed to be. One day, they heard that the wise and respected medicine man, Kwatolo, would soon visit a nearby town to meet with the sick and injured. So, when the day arrived, Hatoto and his parents woke early and took the long journey from their small village. Although the line to meet Kwatolo was longer than the Amazon River, Hatoto and his parents waited patiently beneath the hot sun. Finally, after many, many hours, they stood before the great Kwatolo."

A.J. was so caught up in the tension of the story, she instinctively grabbed my hand and squeezed it. Rather than shake her off, I stayed still, grateful for the comforting contact.

"Please Kwatolo,' Hatoto begged."

While Yazzie delivered the narration in his deep, husky tone, Halana acted out the dialogue, altering her voice every time a different character spoke.

She continued in Hatoto's sad and pleading voice, "all my life, my legs have failed me. They are weak and broken. For ten years, my parents have carried me but now I am grown, and my father is tired, my mother is sick, and I need your guidance. Please!"

"With that Hatoto's mother cried out. Though she tried to stay strong, she feared that Kwatolo might not have the answer."

Hatoto's mother wasn't the only one waiting with bated breath. The corners of my eyes moistened as I prayed for the happy ending this poor family deserved.

"My child," Kwatolo spoke in a frail but knowing whisper, "the question is hard, but the answer is simple. When you lie down amongst the dancing grass, you shall find the strength you need."

"With that, the wise doctor moved on to the next person waiting in line, but Hatoto still had many questions,"

"But where is the field? How will I know how to find it?" Hatoto wondered while his mother sobbed loudly behind him.

"My child," Kwatolo replied, "you shall find it where the sky and the earth flow together," he added before turning back to his next patient.

"Hatoto and his parents were crestfallen. They were sure their journey home would be one that they could, for the first time, walk together. With his mother too sick and too tired to help, Hatoto's father had no choice but to carry his son the entire journey home. After hours of walking, Hatoto's father needed to rest so he stopped and lay his son down for a moment by the side of the road. As the disheartened boy lay there, a sudden gust breezed by, making the grass around him swing and sway."

"As Hatoto lifted his head to the sky, an astonishing vision struck him; a vision of him dancing in the grass, swinging and swaying to the rhythm of the breeze."

"Father! Father! Look! Look! Can't you see me dancing?" Hatoto cried, but his father did not share his vision.

"Mother! Mother! Look! Look! Do you see me dancing?" the frenzied boy asked though the answer was the same.

"As the family finally arrived home, everyone in their village rushed to learn of Hatoto's visit to the medicine man, but while his mother and father wore expressions of sadness and exhaustion, Hatoto wore one of glee."

"While I lay in the field, the wind blew strong, and the grass began to dance, and when I looked up, I saw myself in the sky, dancing a most wonderful dance. My legs - they were strong and powerful and moved with the wind."

"As he spoke, Hatoto felt a strange and sudden tingle in his legs. The more he spoke, the more they tingled and the more they tingled, the more he spoke until his legs felt so strong and sturdy, he stood before the watching crowd. No longer needing to describe his vision, the jubilant boy danced while his parents fell before his feet, weeping tears of joy. While he danced, the village joined him, step by step, sway by sway and today in our culture, we celebrate Hatoto's miracle with the Grass Dance. And now it's your turn!" Yazzie announced before fetching a large basket from the hallway.

Though dressing up in the regalia was optional, A.J. and I were first to volunteer as the kaleidoscope of colour was so utterly enchanting.

First, we squeezed our feet into soft, deerskin moccasins before pulling the most beautiful cotton jingle dresses over our heads and down over our drab, grey uniforms. The mint green and electric orange swirls adorning mine made me look like I was blanketed by a thousand exotic butterflies. Shining shells and soft feathers hung from my dress like prized trophies. **Dismal Air** had crash-landed, and **Pow Wow Air** was ready for take-off! I vowed to wear my pow-wow dress forever (or at least until break time).

"Let me help you with your roaches," Halana offered while I bowed my head low enough for her to reach (I was such an awkwardly tall child.)

The roach was a beaded orange headband with two eagle feathers proudly protruding from my ponytail. When Yazzie held up a mirror for me to see this wild-west ensemble, it looked like I had grown two fluffy antennae.

"You are almost ready but before we start, no Native American can Pow-Wow dance without their eagle feather fan."

As Yazzie handed out the fans, Halana pressed play on the YouTube video and invited all of us to follow her lead.

"Remember if you move to the right, you must then move to the left. If you swing your arm left, you must then swing it back to the right. The grass dance is all about balance," Yazzie instructed while hopping and spinning amongst us all.

Jarvis couldn't resist making a fuss: stumbling and staggering about before promptly giving up without trying. Sebastian quickly put him in his place,

"I'm sure if a meerkat can tap-dance, a genius like you can spin in a circle!" he jested with a wry smile that seemed to do the trick.

Briefly abandoning their eternal quest to be (and stay) cool, all the boys threw on porcupine head roaches and got involved although one or two couldn't help but slap their palm against their lips to chant, "AW-WA-WA-WA, AW-WA-WA-WA."

As the soft, patterned pop of the drum pulsed through me and the high-pitched wail drowned out my surroundings, for the first time in forever, I felt lost. Good lost. Completely lost in a moment. Shells jangled and ribbons swayed while limbs of different lengths veered in unfamiliar directions. Clock hands froze and a surge of supercharged happiness pulsed through me, to the very edge of my fingernails. Even my eyelashes felt giddy.

Every time I spun, a carousel of smiling faces whirled past, but A.J.'s grin was grander than them all. As we turned and stomped, all our worries vanished like chocolate chip cookies fresh from the oven.

"Imagine this had been my first day at school number four", I thought to myself, "please let Mr Blafferty's "temporary" absence be as long as one of his ranking assemblies."

My oblivion was punctuated by a brief and unexpected glimpse of Mrs Mayhew standing in the doorway, nodding and smiling at everyone who caught her eye.

As the drumbeat eased, Mrs Murphy clapped her dust-covered hands and brought everyone to a halt,

"Well I've never seen such wonderful dancing," she beamed, "I think Hatoko would be so pleased with your efforts," she mistakenly added.

Though I felt an immediate urge to correct her error, my first word in over three years was not going to be used to embarrass someone else.

"Can we carefully remove all the dresses and headbands and please give Yazzie and Halana a huge round of applause?" she asked.

I would have loved nothing more than to run up and tell Halana and Yazzie how much I adored the story of Hatoto and how I wanted to Pow-Wow dance every day for the rest of my life. But I didn't. I couldn't.

As everyone waved goodbye and ran out for break-time, I hung back, pushed my fingers into my ears and breathed a sigh of relief. With no study hall to hibernate in, I hovered near A.J., trying to digest all the noise and madness going on around me.

Ridiculous rumours buzzed about that Mr

Blafferty was caught stealing three bunches of organic green grapes from Waitrose. Another wild theory also speculated that he had been summoned to Buckingham Palace by the Queen, who was keen to learn all about his revolutionary SMARP machine. Bradley canvassed the entire playground trying to persuade everyone that the meerkat was indeed remote controlled as he had spotted Mrs Mayhew stuffing something furry into a box before locking it in a cupboard under the stage.

In the remaining workshops, we explored the traditional dances of Ireland, New Zealand, Brazil and India and while they were all enjoyable, none came close to recreating the magic and energy of our Pow-Wow session. During lunch, some of the older boys got particularly sweaty and shouty as they tried (with limited success) to recreate the Haka.

The girls preferred to invent their own mish-mash routine made up of Irish, Bhangra and Samba dancing. For the entirety of the school day, music and stories, dancing and laughter filled the classrooms and corridors of Thrive Academy. When the pick-up parents arrived outside the gates at 3.30 to collect their usually hungry and deflated children, they were startled by the tidal wave of,

"Mum! Mum! I can Irish dance, watch!"

"Dad! Dad! The New Zealand rugby dance is really rude!"

"Mum! Dad! Mrs Mayhew has a pet squirrel that does strictly come dancing!"

When my dad arrived home that evening, he didn't have to ask how my day was. He could tell from my eyes and my smile that something strange and wonderful had happened.

Four million texts were just about enough to give him a blow by blow account of my BEST SCHOOL DAY EVER!

7

Slam Dunk Day

Nobody in the history of the world had ever looked forward to a Tuesday. But I couldn't wait.

Thanks to STINKIN' SCREAMIN' RUBBISH HOLE's new, super-speedy Wi-Fi, I was able to text dad every last detail of my day without using up all my 4G. Every time he text back, the shocked emojis grew in number.

Miz Mayhew has a dancin meerkat

😨

Wen she danced her laces lookd like butterflies

😨😨

Hatoto cudnt walk n then he had a vision

😨😨😨

We got 2 dress up & Pow-Wow dance

😬😬😬😬

I smiled so much I thawt my face wz goin 2 crack.

😬😬😬😬😬

When I text dad at seven pm to tell him I was off to bed, his own face transformed into a shocked emoji. But I wasn't demanding a first class ticket to the Land of Nod because I was tired, I simply could not wait for the sequel to Mrs Mayhew's magical assembly. I scrubbed my face and hands so well, I feared dad might struggle to recognise me when he arrived to tuck me in. When he leaned down to kiss me goodnight, my perfectly brushed teeth almost blinded him,

"Woah, have you had diamonds implanted in your gums?" he joked before kissing the top of my forehead, "I need to find out what Mrs Mayhew's trick is because whatever it is, it's working. Ehmm, do you wear a golden tie?" he suddenly asked.

I shook my head and pointed to the grey and blue snake hanging from the back of my desk chair with the rest of my uniform.

"I got an email from the school explaining her appointment, and they've said she wants everyone wearing the same tie," dad explained before retreating towards the unexpectedly peaceful evening now awaiting him. (I was sure he'd already planned a mini Game of Thrones binge.)

"Oh, and it also said that everyone must bring a packed lunch as they're closing the canteen for the day. No reason given so she must have something strange up her sleeve for tomorrow!" dad predicted before clicking my light off and skipping downstairs.

As I lay there in the dark wondering what exactly she had "up her sleeve", I was filled with so much excitement, it felt like Christmas Eve. I set my alarm clock for 7am along with two extra alarms set five and ten minutes later just in case. After a few verses of mum's lullaby, the Sandman came calling.

Though he no longer needed to walk me to the school gate, dad still insisted,

"I'm not taking the risk of you skipping school like you did before," he warned in an unusually stern tone.

There was more chance of Jurassic Park being real than me ever wanting to play truant on that Tuesday. As we arrived at the school gates, I genuinely thought a theme-park full of re-incarnated dinosaurs had replaced Thrive Academy. Masses of people crowded around the gate, bumping each other with their shoulders and school bags, determined to nudge their way to the front. Passers-by must have assumed that a prize-winning author or a record-breaking athlete was making a special visit.

At 8.55, the gates opened but the vomity-choking noise didn't come - the pig must have phoned in sick. Our second surprise arrived when we entered the assembly hall; the turnstiles had vanished.

"Blafferty will restore them the instant he

returns," Jarvis Bonson declared while staggering through the unusually open space.

Instead of his "special" tie, the golden boy was wearing a disgruntled frown. The hall was alive with panicked-breath and nerve-shredding excitement. Those brown, plastic seats felt extra bumpy and extra uncomfortable as nobody could sit still. No matter how many times we looked towards the assembly hall clock, its hands seemed to tick by at a deliberately unhurried pace.

Mr Wingman was nowhere to be seen, and Bradley was already spreading stories,

"Wingman walked into his office yesterday evening and found that dancing monkey sitting in his swivel chair. He tried to get him out, but the furball wouldn't move. Instead, he just handed Wingman a piece of paper that said, 'U R FIRED!' Mr Wingman was so shocked, he just walked out, and as he did, he noticed that the sign on the door which had, for eight years, read Mr Wingman, now read Mr Paradisi."

Of course, this was likely just another of Bradley's wild rumours. A far simpler explanation for Mr Wingman's sudden departure was entirely possible but if it was simple then it was probably super-dull, and Bradley wasn't going to let the truth get in the way of a good story.

Mrs Mayhew's second assembly was a guinea-pig's teardrop away, and the mouths around me speculated wildly about what today's extravaganza might be, "No way will it top yesterday!" Bradley declared, "and I bet she's bought new batteries for her remote-control rat!"

"I hope she's trained an orangutan how to play guitar," A.J yearned.

"I'm all for entertainment as long as it has some educational value," Sebastian grumbled.

As the clock reluctantly trickled towards 9 am, Mr Paradisi (as he was now known) wandered along the edge of the stage bouncing a mini basketball.

"So fake!" Bradley tutted in disgust.

On the fifth bounce, the blue curtains whipped back, and there stood Mrs Mayhew. Green was gone. Red was in. Her spectacles, ribbon laces, blouse buttons and pleated skirt were all the colour of homemade strawberry jam. Shining, silver butterflies clung to the bottom lobe of each ear while a dainty, pearl necklace drooped around the top of her chest. A thick, red hair-band made her digestive biscuit hair seem like it was smiling.

Though I was curious about the change in colour, I was even more intrigued by the small trampoline and the full-size basketball net which filled the left side of the stage. At the base of the hoop sat a ragged net bag stuffed with mini-basketballs which looked like they'd been plucked from the Pacific by an enormous fishing trawler.

Before Mrs Mayhew spoke, a balding, middle-aged man, clutching a clipboard, walked out onto the stage. After clearing his throat, the visitor croaked, "Good morning children ... I am Mr Chuck Clyst ... the chief validator ... from the Office ... of World Records ... and today ... I am here to verify ... whether or not ... your head-teacher ... Mrs Mayhew can dunk ... seventy-five basketballs ... in under eight minutes."

Chuck Clyst had the slowest speaking voice in history. His speech was slower than one of Mr Blafferty's ranking assemblies. Rumours swirled that he could roll off the alphabet in just under 3.5 months.

"The current..." he continued sleepily, "... world record ... stands at seventy-four...and has remained ... unbroken for fifteen years. Her, eh ... assistant, Mr Paradisi ... will bounce the balls into the...air which she must ... catch and then ... clearly dunk inside ... the hoop. Before we ... set the clock...one more adjustment ... is required."

On this mark, Mr Paradisi scuttled up the pole, fetched a lighter from underneath his top hat and set the hoop alight.

"Red light, red light!" Sebastian screamed

Aloud causing the *insensitives* around him to titter. Quickly spotting his distress, Mrs Murphy swooped in to comfort him.

With the flaming circle glowing above her head, Mrs Mayhew lowered her lightly rouged bottom lip and sang a similar but slightly different song to the day before,

"May you always live your life,
may you soar to greater heights.
May you always love your life,
may you crawl, then walk, then fly."

Again the song ended rather abruptly. After yesterday, we should have expected it, but it still felt so strange. Strolling to the far side of the stage, she stretched out her arms and kicked off her shoes while a sea of eyes looked on in stunned silence.

"The clock ... will begin .... when you score ... your first basket," Chuck Clyst clarified at a sluggish snail's pace.

Suddenly, our little head-teacher sprinted for the hoop. She started with such a ferocious speed that a few of us hopped in our chairs with fright. Into the taut rubber she *boinged* before catapulting through the air. As she flew, Mr Paradisi smashed a basketball into the ground which sprung towards her hands, perfectly placed for her to catch it. Firmly and confidently, she grasped the ball and crashed it through the flaming circle of fire.

"One!" confirmed Mr Clyst, slightly spooked by the speed at which Mrs Mayhew sprinted past him to get back to her starting position.

"Seventy...four...to... go!" he added.

"She'll never do it!" grumbled Bradley.

"I bet she will!" hoped A.J.

"She'll burn her fingers," feared Sebastian.

Mrs Mayhew was shooting over and back the stage like a dizzy firework, but after sixty seconds, she had only dunked eight balls. Although I was no *mathamagician*, I quickly calculated that if she dunked eight baskets in one minute, then she would only dunk sixty-four baskets in eight minutes and miss out on the world record (possibly even less because she'd be so exhausted by the end.)

Someone sitting near the front must have also done some quick mind-maths because they suddenly jumped to their feet and yelled,

"Come on Mrs Mayhew! Smash that record!"

This helpful yelp burst the bubble of open-mouthed silence and inspired the rest of the assembly hall to cheer our tiny head-teacher. As another sixty seconds ticked by, our support was speeding Mrs Mayhew up.

Nineteen slam dunks down.

Fifty-six to go.

With six minutes remaining, Mr Paradisi bounced the balls as swiftly as his little furry fingers would allow. Although her face was reddening and her breathing was growing heavier, nothing could stop her, she was slamming them in with passion and precision.

36. Slam!

37. Smash!

38. Bang!

39. Whack!

40. Boom!

Three minutes remained. Thirty-five more slam dunks to break the world record.

"How can she do it? It's impossible!" I thought to myself before a girl sitting behind me suddenly stood up.

"Take off your necklace miss!" she yelled through cupped hands. "It'll help you jump higher; it's weighing you down!"

Mrs Mayhew offered a big thumbs up as she whipped off her pearls and sent them flying towards Mr Paradisi who leaned his little head to the right and caught them around his neck like a hula-hooping legend.

"I was going to say that about the necklace," A.J. whispered with a frustrated look upon her face.

The little girl's small suggestion made a big difference; Mrs Mayhew was now quicker and more aerodynamic than before.

48. Bam!

49. Wham!

50. Kaboom!

Twenty-five slam-dunks stood between her and that world record but only two minutes remained. Another student shot up from their chair, but this time they were not planning on shouting advice. The little girl, who must have been in Year 3, darted to the front of the assembly hall stage and threw something towards Mrs Mayhew.

"Here miss, take my bobble! Tie your hair back, and you will be even faster!"

The relentless slam-dunker offered another thumbs up in appreciation. Twisting the hair-tie, she fixed her sweating mop into a pony-tail. Yet another small change to how she approached the launch pad meant she ran faster and flew further into the air.

60. Bash!

61. Crash!

62. No!

"Red light! Red light!" Sebastian bellowed.

Somehow, she'd missed: she'd bounced too high and got too close to the flaming hoop. As she fanned her hand through the air and winced, everyone could see her pain but we could also tell from her eyes that there was no way she was giving up.

One minute left. Fourteen baskets left. Fourteen slam-dunks to smash the world record.

You could tell from Mr Clyst's expression that he felt this latest attempt was over - done for. In fifteen years, he had likely seen many fail. However, I couldn't let this marvellous woman fail. Not when her enormous efforts had got her so close.

I had to do something, and an idea had been bouncing around my head. The urge to speak was greater than ever, but my mouth was so dry and my tongue was so blunt, there was no way I could do it. Reaching for my bag, I grabbed my butterfly notebook and scribbled something.

A.J. was the first to notice what I was doing. Before I'd even finished jotting my message, she stood up and screamed towards the stage,

"Dunk two at a time! It's the only way!"

I have no idea how he understood, but Mr Paradisi instantly grabbed and slammed two basketballs, one with each hand into the ground. Mrs Mayhew, without her pearls and with her biscuit hair tied back, leapt through the air, seized one basketball in her left hand and clutched the other in her right. With perfect timing and flawless precision, she sank them both, one after the other.

"Sixty-six!" a group of students roared harmoniously, drowning out Mr Clyst's tepid count-up.

Thirty seconds remained.

Up she went again, spinning through the air like a dazzling, dizzying Catherine Wheel. With both hands full, that hoop was in her sights.

"Sixty-eight!" bawled the mathematical choir.

Twenty seconds left...

Despite doubting her at first, Bradley was now as involved as everyone else; willing her to succeed; shouting louder than anyone.

"Seventy!" screeched everyone (except me) with an excitement that the walls of the hall could hardly contain. We were stamping our feet, pumping our fists. This had to happen, but time was running out. Mrs Mayhew's energy levels were low but everyone could see that she would never surrender. With just fifteen seconds left, she only had time to make two more runs at the hoop which meant a maximum of four more slam-dunks.

"It won't be enough," Sebastian shrieked, chewing all five nails on his right hand at once.

"Seventy-two!" roared the crowd.

With just eight seconds left, we knew that the attempt was doomed. Mrs Mayhew only had enough time for one final run at the hoop.

"What a shame," I thought to myself, "she's tried so hard."

Without warning, Bradley suddenly shot up out of his seat, cupped his right hand around his mouth and bellowed,

"BOUNCE THREE!"

"But she can't catch three. She's only got two hands!" argued the boy sitting next to him.

"We have to try!" Bradley wailed, now completely consumed by his head teacher's quest.

Scooping three basketballs out of the fishnet bag, Mr Paradisi, whisked them furiously, one after another, into the air while Mrs Mayhew made her final ascent.

Everyone was now on their feet, their eyes and mouths wider than ever before. With her right hand, she caught the first ball. With her left hand, she snatched the second before this exhausted little woman somehow pushed the two basketballs towards one another and wedged the third ball in between them to create the world's first basketball sandwich.

Three seconds...

She was so close but how would she get three balls in one hoop?

Two...

Rapidly rotating her arms, she stacked the three basketballs vertically like a triple-layer chocolate-orange cake.

One...

She let them go as the entire hall inhaled one enormous, collective gasp. With a crash, she fell to the floor and skidded along the wooden planks, scraping her little, bony knees. Nobody cheered. Nobody chanted. Frantic heads flickered left then right,

"Has she done it? Has she done it?" A.J. screamed while flinging her limbs about like she was Pow-Wow dancing.

We had to know. We needed someone to nod or smile or do something - anything to put us out of our misery. But blank faces abounded. Nobody said anything. Everyone wondered, "has she done it in time?" Mrs Mayhew had given her all, and with a little help from the crowd, she had come so close. But had she come close enough?

Tapping his pen upon the top of his clipboard, Chuck Clyst shuffled forward. Some might have thought he was intentionally trying to build up suspense, but this man only had one setting: slug slow.

"Today ... your head-teacher ... Mrs Mayhew has ... in under eight minutes, dunked ... seventy ... five ... basketballs."

The entire hall went bananas!

Absolutely bananas!

The deafening noise didn't just lift the roof off; it literally lifted the building's foundations from the ground as if the entire hall was a secret spaceship about to take off on a special mission to Mars.

"She did it!" squealed Bradley.

"She smashed it!" screamed A.J.

"I've gone deaf!" worried Sebastian.

Mr Paradisi dashed towards his dance partner, scampered up her arm and gave her whole head the biggest, squeeziest hug. Joining in, we all hugged and high-fived everyone within reaching distance until the record-breaking head teacher stepped to the edge of the stage. After a few moments, the hall fell silent and she opened her mouth to sing the same four lines as before. Although they weren't exactly the same because this time, the words meant something and a handful of students felt compelled to join in.

"May you always live your life,

may you soar to greater heights.

May you always love your life,

may you crawl, then walk, then fly."

Right on cue, the clock struck nine fifteen and morning assembly was over.

On Monday, I had heard about the miracle of Hatoto, but on Tuesday, with my very own eyes, I witnessed the eye-popping, jaw-dropping miracle of Mrs Mayhew.

8

World's Tallest Cake?

The rest of Tuesday was super barmy bonkers.

As we filed out of the assembly hall, a gigantic chalkboard stopped us in our tracks. Scratches of pink chalk posed a fascinating question,

"Which world record will
you smash today?"

Beneath this query, someone had written a delicious menu full of mouth-watering challenges (quite literally) waiting for us to get our teeth into.

Can you chomp 11 crackers in 60 seconds?
Can you scoff 25 marshmallows in under a minute?
How much jelly can you eat with chopsticks?
How many t-shirts can you wear in 2 minutes?
Who can type the alphabet on an iPad in 10 seconds?

Everyone gathered around 'oohing' and 'aahing' about which records they were going to smash.

"That's so easy!"

"How is that even a record?"

"I could do that in my sleep!"

While everyone was feeling confident about obliterating any and every world record ever set, they weren't quite so sure about where this "smashing" was going to take place.

"Do we go to our classrooms like yesterday?" Tabitha Guild wondered aloud.

"No Tabby, look! It says everyone must go to the sports hall," Benedict Uddin clarified.

"But Benny, we don't have a sports hall," she corrected.

"Oh yeah," Benedict spat while spinning and scanning his eyes around the school yard, entirely perplexed by where this mysterious building might be.

"Do you think she means the study hall?" he added.

"Let's go see!" Tabitha suggested as a gang of fifty followed her vapour trail. It had been so long since sport (or movement of any kind) had been timetabled at Thrive Academy that my oblivious classmates hadn't noticed the faded basketball court markings beneath their study hall desks. Nor had they spotted the holes in the wall which used to house the screws that kept the basketball hoops upright or the hooks that once held the badminton nets straight.

Near the bottom of the chalkboard menu, I spotted something particularly appetising: an all-day option that truly tickled my taste buds. Rather than rotate around the different stations in the sports hall, we could spend the entire day on one super-sized record attempt.

"Can you bake the world's tallest cake?"

"Are you thinking what I'm thinking?" A.J. asked, spotting the direction of my gaze.

A quick shake of my head was the starting pistol that sent us sprinting for the canteen where the lead cook, Miss Patton and her three assistants, Matt, Sandy and Sue all waited.

"It abso-toot-ely must have a layer of rocky road!" A.J. insisted while I agreed with a double thumbs up and a theatrical grin.

As we and approximately thirty others gathered inside the double doors of the canteen, Miss Patton began her drill routine,

"Now you lot might think you're up to this but be warned - this will be your first and only record attempt of the day!"

Because I always brought a packed lunch, I'd never encountered Miss Patton or even sat in the school canteen. But I'd heard rumours that if you hesitated for a split-second to say 'please' or 'thank you', she would ruin your weekend with a five page essay outlining "The Ten Joys of Salad."

If it wasn't typed in Times New Roman, font size 12, double spaced and in her hand by 9 am on Monday, you ran the risk of double bubble: "The Twenty Joys of Vegetables."

While she was short on height, she was stuffed with scary. Her "welcome" was so loud and so stern, I instinctively felt compelled to say "please lovely lady" and "thank you kind woman" even though she hadn't done anything for me.

"This will take all day and bagfuls of sweat and dedication. If you think you can slink away after an hour to shove forty thousand jelly beans up your nose-holes, you better think again. This record attempt will take commitment, patience," she suddenly paused, "and about fourteen million sprinkles!"

Though none of us knew how to react, her face suddenly broke into a mile-wide-smile while Matt, Sandy and Sue fell about laughing.

"I'm only kidding. If we are going to build the world's tallest cake, we will only succeed if we have tonnes of fun along the way. So, who's with me?" she roared before hauling a bag of flour larger than a chubby toddler up from the floor.

Everyone's hands shot up. Miss Patton now had a strong team made up of all years and genders who were ready and impatient to begin.

"The current world record stands at nine point one feet which is roughly the size of a hotel Christmas tree so we must make sure our bottom tier is wider and thicker than a tractor tyre. Seeing as we don't own an oven big enough to bake a tractor tyre, we will have to bake roughly thirty regular sized cakes, place them all in a circle, fill that circle with more cakes and then fill in the spaces between the cakes with smaller pieces of chopped up cake. And because we're only permitted eight hours to complete our challenge, we must be done by three-fifteen."

My ears were open, but my mouth was full of saliva. If I had unfastened it even a smidge, a waterfall of drool would have poured from my lips.

Mum and I loved to bake. Whenever she wasn't working or painting, we were baking, and butterfly cupcakes were our speciality. While mum did all the measuring, mixing, scalping the tops off the buns and cutting them in half to create the butterfly wings, it was my job to plop a dollop of icing on top and wedge the wings in. A little shake of icing sugar and they were ready to be devoured. Since mum died, I've had to rely on #instabake and #cakesofinstagram to satisfy my sweet tooth because dad has the culinary expertise of a university student who forgets to remove the packaging when warming up sausage rolls.

After a quick demonstration from Miss Patton, we began making our own sponge cakes.

Cracking!

Shaking!

Mixing!

Slopping!

With exactly thirty cakes needed to make the base, everyone knew the stakes involved, and nobody wanted to let the team down. Quite quickly, we realised our different strengths and weaknesses: some of us were strong enough to stir the cake mix just right while others could crack eggs like a ninja baker. Despite being an expert mixer, I was far too clumsy to break an egg in two. Every egg I cracked ended up in a zillion gooey pieces until A.J. took over.

Once the mix was ready, we carefully poured it into our circular tins before placing them in a long line along the counter top; ready and waiting to enter the four industrial ovens. While the sponge cake bases waited, Miss Patton taught us the next step,

"Now listen up everyone, while tier one will be covered in pre-rolled sugar icing to make it strong and sturdy, the next tier will be a triple-decker double-chocolate fudge cake covered with sprinkles!"

I made a noise.

From my mouth.

It just fell out. It wasn't a word or a scream. It was some sort of weird "oorgghh" that sounded like a pelican drooling. Everyone stared towards A.J. and me, searching for the origin of this slow and peculiar peli-drool. Though my face blushed red, A.J. kindly intervened,

"Soz, guys that was me – oorgghh!" she lied, recreating the sound to cover my shame which this time made everyone laugh, "the very mention of chocolate cake and sprinkles does strange things to me," she rambled on convincingly.

I was still so thrown by the unexpected peli-drool that I had to step outside for a moment. As I rushed through the doors, wiping my sticky hands along my apron, the light breeze cooled my furnace face. Once I plugged my ears with my fingers, mum's angelic hymn soothed my anxious breath.

"Are you ... alright, Willow?" a kind voice asked though I only caught the final few words. As I unplugged my fingers and looked around, I was startled to find Mrs Mayhew staring back.

"Don't worry Miss," A.J. assured as she arrived to intervene yet again, "we just discovered we're allowed to eat the cake after we smash the world record and I think it was too much excitement for *SOME* of us."

Mrs Mayhew laughed while A.J. laced her arm through mine and led me back towards the cake factory.

Fifty minutes later, the most delicious chocolate icing I'd ever tasted in my life coated my fingers. While of course, we swore we'd never lick our spatulas, the moment Miss Patton kneeled down to pop a waiting cake into the oven; we licked them clean. Everyone was so in harmony. We were like synchronised lickers - Olympic standard. After years of looking at pictures of cakes on my phone (that looked so delicious I was (almost) tempted to lick the screen) I simply had no willpower left.

"Keep going, gang. We'll all be world record holders by this afternoon!" Miss Patton encouraged as she shut an oven door.

By 10.45, it was time for a short break, but nobody wanted to pause the action. Even toilet breaks were kept to a minimum although this did result in some severe leg crossing until people finally surrendered and scurried to the loos.

While Tier Two baked, half the team carried our warm Tier One cakes over to a large table in the corner of the canteen. After they positioned every sumptuous sponge cake into a wondrously wide circle, Matt, Sandy and Sue covered them all with thick, pre-rolled sugar icing. The other half, including A.J. and I (who had been secretly awarded Star Bakers by Miss Patton) were now mixing up a chocolate biscuit mix for Tier Three.

There are many joys in life but for me, mixing cracked Maltesers with crushed digestives and squishy mini-marshmallows (not forgetting the tinchiest pinch of dried fruit) with my bare (scrub-washed ☺) hands was glorious. If I could flop into a bean bag and spend the rest of my days licking that irresistible mix clean from my fingers, I would die happy. Thankfully Miss Patton was there to obstruct such feverish daydreams and keep us focused.

"Make sure you level out on top and press down the biscuit mix to avoid any air gaps but do pile it higher than Everest. We must reach that record height!" she instructed while waltzing around helping where she could.

"This tier will go into our walk-in fridge, so they get cold and congeal. As none of you have even hinted at needing a break-time snack, I assume you are all sneaking samples of our work so I think we should take five before Tier Three begins."

Right on cue, Mrs Mayhew and Mrs Murphy arrived with trays of orange squash and plates of biscuits.

"Ooh a digestive," A.J. whispered in panto-sarcasm, "it's been decades since I've had a digestive."

Though we had secretly nibbled the odd crumb or three, we still chomped and slurped away merrily while the visiting teachers inspected our morning's work.

"Looks like we might well beat the record!" Mrs Murphy enthused while Mrs Mayhew smiled.

A week earlier, I was trapped in a silent study hall struggling to remember the difference between longitude and latitude, and now I was surrounded by giggles, covered in cake mix and consumed by the feeling that today might be the most extraordinary day.

Tier Four was carrot cake, and even though the tiers were getting narrower as our creation grew skyward, Miss Patton still insisted we still made one each as she had a rather ingenious plan,

"When your carrot cakes are ready, I'm going to put extra thick butter icing along the top and then double-decker each cake which I hope will help us gain an extra foot or two. We've only four hours left, so we better get mixing!"

Spinning and stirring and stirring and spinning; I rotated my wrists faster than a spin dry washing machine. I was so rapid I was sure I'd end up with big muscly Popeye arms. The carrot cake wasn't quite as much fun as the biscuit cake but I was so full of Malteser crumbs and digestive biscuits, I was able to resist my sneaky-licky-finger urges.

By lunchtime, four delicious tiers were baked, chilled and stacked and for the first time, Miss Patton pulled out a measuring tape to check our progress. Everyone crossed their fingers (while a few still crossed their legs – toilet break delay tactics!)

"Willow, seeing as you're the tallest, would you mind holding the ladder please and grip the bottom of the tape measure while I pull it up."

While it still felt slightly strange being called by my name instead of a two or three digit number, to be entrusted with such a responsibility filled me with delight.

"One foot ... two feet ... three ... four ... four-point-five... ooh, just short of five," she announced, causing a collective and deflated "aww" to slip from our lips, "we still have a few feet to grow."

Suddenly wave of indigestion rose

through me. Serious indigestion. With only two hours left, our chances of success were tinier than Tom Thumb's dandruff.

"Can we work through lunch and keep going miss?" a little girl with a flour covered face inquired.

"Well Viktoria, I think that's a marvellous idea, but I'm not sure everyone else is willing to sacrifice their play time. Anyone else happy to keep going?" the head chef inquired.

"YES MISS!!" everyone roared in unison while I nodded furiously like an over-excited woodpecker.

"What amazing little soldiers we have here today. To save time, I want you all to recall the recipe for the strawberry jam sponge cake we made first thing this morning, but just like Mrs Mayhew in her assembly, we are going to need to dunk with both hands!"

A flash of confusion wrinkled many brows.

"Are we baking basketballs Miss?" a bewildered Year 1 tot asked while everyone, including Miss Patton, tried their best not to laugh.

"No! No! Bless you, Maisie. I need you all to stir two bowls at once: one with your right and the other with your left. Otherwise, we're never going to hit that target! And if anyone's struggling, you all know who our master mixer is so just ask Willow for help," Miss Patton commented with a little wink made just for me.

Clouds of flour billowed across the kitchen while A.J. ran around cracking eggs with laser-beam precision.

"We're going to be world record holders just like Mrs M!" A.J. squealed while I whipped the contents of her bowl into a cyclone.

By 2.30, I was yet again holding the ladder as Miss Patton carefully lifted the freshly baked sponge cakes into position.

"Eh, we have a bit of a problem," she announced, triggering a flock of heads to jolt her way. "I'm not tall enough to reach the top."

The indigestion re-awoke within my stomach as I sensed the six words crawling up Miss Patton's throat,

"Willow, could you do it please?"

My knees shook, and my hands trembled as I placed my right foot upon the ladder. While I depended on eight silver steps to prevent gravity pulling me to the floor, everyone else was depending on ten-year-old me to keep their world record hopes alive.

Pressure? What pressure!

Reaching my sweaty palms downwards, I leaned into the ladder and carefully eased the sugar- topped, golden circles from Miss Paton's grasping hands and swivelled right to place them upon our wobbling tower of sponge. I was so sure that I was about to destroy everyone's hard work that I could visualise my first day at School #5 just over the horizon.

"That's it, Willow - nice and gently," Miss Patton calmly assured.

One by one, I placed each cake where they needed to be while everyone below held their breath each time I eased my hand away. Finally, I was done. Our hopes were still intact.

"Right gang," Miss Patton announced, holding out a hand to help me down the ladder. "Despite our best efforts, that puts us at seven feet which means we are still two feet short with less than an hour to go. Even if you mix with both hands and a wooden spoon clamped between your teeth, I honestly don't think we can make it. Unless someone can think of a solution. Any bright ideas?" she shouted over the sound of Maisie and one or two others sniffling and whimpering.

The biting reality of defeat was sinking in. All the suggestions to help Mrs Mayhew in morning assembly had run us dry. We were out of options.

"Could we not take a picture and Photoshop it?" one rather clever (and dubious) character proposed.

"What about driving to Waitrose and buying all their cakes?" another deep-pocketed genius suggested.

Wiping my hands in my apron, I went to fetch my bag. With my wobbling left hand, I furiously scribbled while A.J. shadowed my shoulder, poised to translate my letters into sounds,

"We ... should ... add ... wings!" A.J. announced in a confused tone.

Silence enveloped the kitchen. Nobody seemed to understand. I briefly considered explaining it myself but the instant I considered speaking, my mouth dried and my heart pounded.

I continued to scribble, " ... we make two more cakes ... one big cake ... narrow but tall... then one small cake ... wide but flat ... we cut the second cake ... into pointed triangles ... like wings ... which will give us the height we need."

"A butterfly cupcake!" Miss Patton screeched as everyone finally visualised what I was trying to describe.

"That's brilliant Willow! If we squirt a mini mountain of buttercream icing onto the top of the first cake and then stick the wings into that, we might just have a chance."

Whimpers turned to smiles as the entire kitchen suddenly burst back to life,

"Quickly A.J.! Crack those eggs! Willow! Get mixing!" Miss Patton roared like a sergeant major in the world's first militarised baking unit, "The rest of you start cutting up butter and dishing out the flour; we need to make sure these last two cakes are nothing short of perfection!"

Eggs! Flour! Butter! Elbow grease!

Crack! Puff! Plop! Stir!

"Maisie, can you please keep an eye on that clock and update us every five minutes? We must not lose track of time."

"On it Miss!" Maisie shouted as she set her eyes on both hands of the clock and didn't blink for the remainder of the day, "Forty-five minutes left Miss!"

"We need to get these in the oven now gang. If we don't, we'll never have enough time to shape the wings and get it up there."

"Maybe the wings will be magic, and it will fly up there." A.J. gasped as everyone around her laughed.

While the cakes baked, we prepared the ladder and measured our latest attempt. The cake was precisely 7.3ft, meaning we required a further 2ft, just to be certain.

"Fifteen minutes left!" Maisie screamed without turning her head towards us.

"Right, let's get them out," Miss Patton instructed as Sue grabbed a pair of oven gloves. "A.J., can you fetch Mr Clyst. We need him here to verify our attempt."

While Benedict smothered the top of the taller cake with thick, buttercream icing, I stepped in to cut the wider, thinner cake into wings. Though it had always been mum's job, I knew I could do it. I'd watched her cut them perfectly more than a million times.

"Careful now Willow. If we cut them too thin, they won't stand up," Miss Patton warned.

I wasn't cutting two wings. I was cutting four. Everyone got butterfly buns wrong but mine and mum's were always perfect because we gave our butterflies the four wings they actually had; the larger fore wing and the smaller hind wing.

"Are you doing these little wings as spares?" Miss Patton asked.

I shook my head no without looking her way. I didn't have the tools nor the time to explain. The smaller hind wing was not just me being awkwardly precise; I knew it would help the larger wing stay upright.

"Ten minutes left!" Maisie bellowed moments before good ol' Chuck arrived with his clipboard.

Cutting the wings and wedging them into the icing was reasonably straightforward but lifting these final additions would be far from it.

"A.J., to make it easier, could you follow Willow up the ladder and stop halfway so we can pass them up in stages," Miss Patton thoughtfully suggested.

Poised and petrified, I reached my trembling hands down towards A.J. to collect the final tier.

"Take your time now Willow. We still have a few minutes to spare," Miss Patton assured.

Slowly turning, I reached up as far as I could to make sure the butterfly topper was dead centre and not going to topple over the second I let it go.

All day the kitchen had been awash with mouths giggling and pots banging, but as Chuck replaced me on the ladder and unspooled his measuring tape, nobody dared breathe.

"FIVE MINUTES LEFT!" Maisie suddenly wailed.

Everyone gasped in horror as Maisie's shriek caused Mr Clyst to trip on the third step. An audible gulp promptly followed the gasp as

Mr Trippy Toes mindlessly leaned his left hand on to the edge of Tier 3 to regain his balance. Thankfully the rocky road was sturdy enough to steady the wobbling wally.

"Sorry," Maisie whispered.

Miss Patton reached out to take the end of the tape measure as Chuck unspooled it from the top of the ladder.

"Looks like ... it's ... at least ... four ... five ... ... six," he slowly counted. Tortoise slow.

Instinctively, I grabbed A.J.'s hand and squeezed it.

"Seven ... ... eight," A.J. squeezed me back.

"Nine ... ... nine-point-five feet exactly."

Nobody could believe it.

Everybody screamed!

Cheered!

Whooped!

Hurriedly, Chuck Clyst climbed down the ladder before the sound waves of our screams toppled them both.

"Well done world record breakers or should I say World Record BAKERS!" Miss Patton beamed while offering high fives all around.

"Miss? Miss? Who's going to take it home?" Tabitha asked with a little twinkle in her eye.

"Oh, I haven't even thought about what we'll do with it Tabby. Anyone got any ideas?" she asked.

Again, I turned to my notebook. A.J. was immediately on hand to translate,

"I think we should ... raffle the cake ... for charity."

"Wow! Well that is a fab idea! What do we think gang? Shall we raffle it off and make a tonne of money for charity?" Miss Patton asked.

Everyone nodded in agreement except for Figgy Drizzlecott who manically waved her hands in the air,

"Miss? I don't mind raffling it but will we be allowed to enter?" she selfishly wondered.

"I don't see why not," Miss Patton replied with a little titter, "Willow, seeing as it was your idea, can you suggest a charity?"

Without hesitating, I scratched my pencil into my pad,

"Cancer Research U.K." A.J. announced.

"Oh, of course. A very worthy cause," Miss Patton blushed while a few of the children started to whisper, "I'll create a donation page on Facebook and let everyone know about it."

By the school gate at 3.15, tongues were wagging about ours and everyone else's endeavours. Jarvis Bonson achieved a world record by sticking sixty-five post-it notes to his face. Andy Wood in Year 4 managed to assemble a Mr Potato Head while blindfolded in 16.08 seconds, shaving just 0.9 off the previous world record.

Four world records in one day was not bad for a random Tuesday in March but little did we know that our record-breaking exploits were about to shine a very big spotlight on the very small village of Ickleton.

9

B(re)aking News

That evening, I parked myself in dad's beloved and bedraggled recliner which I was only allowed laze in when he wasn't around. Thankfully, he was busy in the kitchen, wrestling with the wrapping of the pepperoni pizza that would barely feed us both. While he supervised the precarious cheese-melting process through the glass oven door, we text back and forth about another super-crazy day.

Although I sent him a squillion texts, he replied to each one with a little emoji story; he was terrible at texting but cute, colourful symbols seemed to be his thing.

she broke d world record wid sec 2 spare

& burnt her hand on d flamin hoop

🔥😣🏀

we tried 2 beat d world record 4 d biggest cake

😊🎂🏆

But we ran out of time (& flour)

😟💩

Jokes! We did break d record!

😥🏆🎂🎂

we r going 2 raffle it 4 charity

👆💲😊

& I chose Cancer Research UK

👊🤕😦

As it was his turn to pick the Tuesday night film, I braced myself for another night of dungeons and dragons. (Fantasy epics are his fave! His top three are The Princess Bride, Labyrinth and yes, you guessed it, Willow). At one point, he had his heart set on calling me Hoggle (the ugly troll who helps Sarah get baby Toby back from the Goblin King in Labyrinth) but thankfully, my mother had enough sway and sense to remind him that fantasy and reality don't mix.

When dad proudly waltzed in with two plates of expertly thawed out pizza twenty minutes later, I instantly vacated his throne. Flicking on the TV, I was poised to press the Netflix button on the remote when a female voice behind the screen pricked my ears,

"Now we join our education correspondent, Emily Nouveaux, who is reporting live from the village of Ickleton in Suffolk."

Instantly, I jumped from the couch, dropped the remote from my hand and pointed with a wrist-cracking speed at the TV but dad had already heard. Popping the plates upon the coffee table, he increased the volume.

Standing outside the gates of my school with a whiplash smile, Emily Nouveaux leaned into her big, serious microphone and replied,

"Thank you, Eileen. This evening I stand

outside a school that until a few days ago was regarded by many as the school of the future. A school that had earned a one point eight million pound investment for a new, cutting edge assessment programme but on Monday, the school's head-teacher, Mr Blafferty, was unexpectedly suspended and his replacement, Mrs Mayhew, has made quite an entrance!"

As the reporter swivelled to the left, the camera panned in the same direction, and there stood the man with the slowest voice in history.

"I'm delighted to be joined by an officer from the World Record Association, Mr Chuck Clyst, who can tell us more about the amazing events that occurred during this morning's assembly."

Despite prodding her microphone closer to his face, slug-slow Chuck didn't get the hint.

"Mr Clyst, can you tell us what happened?" she prompted.

"Oh ... yes ... this morning ..." he began.

Certain that my pizza would be stone-cold by the time he finished his first sentence, I sat down and scoffed it while soaking up this unexpected newsreel. "... Mrs Mayhew ... dunked seventy-five basketballs ... in less than eight minutes ... making her a world record holder."

Ms Nouveaux was clearly anticipating a little more meat on the bone and seemed a touch irritated as she suddenly swung back towards the camera. Appearing out of nowhere, a rather waspy looking middle-aged woman with a heavily hair-sprayed bonce, was impatiently waiting to have her say. For now, the reporter held the mic,

"... and it wasn't only the new head-teacher who broke a world record today. One group of students baked the world's tallest cake while two students achieved individual records, Andy Wood in year four and Jarvis Bonson in year six. I'm now joined by the mother of a world record breaker, Mrs Felicity Bonson. You must be very proud?" the reporter asked.

"Proud?" she squawked back like a very angry parrot, "Of course, I'm not proud. My boy wants to be a pilot! Sticking post-it notes to his face isn't going to get him into Oxford. Is it? Is it?"

Her question wasn't rhetorical; she wanted an answer.

"Well no, but it's still a n-" Emily didn't get to finish her sentence.

"Before Mr Blafferty left, my son was sitting exams every day and making exceptional progress and after just two days of Mrs Matthews,"

"- Mrs Mayhew," the reporter bravely corrected,

"Whatever! He's not had a single test since last Friday. Five days. It's been five days!"

Part of me assumed this was some sort of joke. Dad certainly found it funny.

"Isn't she that fusspot who lives in that big nest at the top of the hill?" he asked.

The crow continued to caw, "First she

scraps golden ties and now I'm supposed to be happy that my boy's face is big enough to fit sixty five post-its. Well, I never."

As amusing as it was, a small ball of dread began to whir in the pit of my stomach and it wasn't the pepperoni.

"Do you know if and when Mr Blafferty might return?" Emily asked.

"It better be soon!" she raved with a face redder than an angry beetroot, "I demand that the governors reinstate Mr Blafferty while they investigate these ridiculous allegations. Mrs Matthews can dance with monkeys and set world records somewhere else – somewhere more befitting her talents. I already have fifteen signatures on my petition and by morning I shall have at least fifty more," she spat before spinning on her sky-high heels and storming off.

"Dancing with monkeys?" Emily repeated into the camera, "I think there's more to this story than meets the eye, Eileen. I might have to dig a little deeper. Back to you in the studio."

"Uh-oh," dad slurred while chewing on a slightly cremated slice of pepperoni, "looks like things just got interesting round here."

10

Paint! Paint! Fly!

Mum painted butterflies.

Hundreds of butterflies in every shape and colour. On weekday evenings, once dad arrived home from the garage, she left to wait tables at the Flat Iron Steakhouse. While I struggled to survive my daily eight-hour school sentence, mum was anchored to the spare room "studio" swirling and brushing her "flying flowers" to life.

As soon as I escaped school, my primary quest (apart from raiding the biscuit tin) was to scamper into her studio to spy her latest creation. My favourite painting, which now hangs above my bed, is the Blue Morpho: a stunning jet-black butterfly with a striking electric blue flash blinging each wing. Mum's favourite, which she painted a billion times, was the Sylphina Angel; a delicate beauty with transparent black-edged wings and a copper coloured, soft-tip tail.

Travelling through Peru to witness them and paint them with her own eyes instead of fuzzy screenshots from Google images was one of mum's many unfulfilled dreams. Shortly before she died, one wish did come true; her very own art exhibition attended by all our friends and family. The GX gallery on Denmark Street in London displayed fifty of her most striking paintings. Because mum was in the middle of treatments, Doctor Morgan advised against her attending. But while her body was weak, her conviction was strong, and a fifty-foot wave couldn't have stopped her from reaching the front door of that gallery.

I remember the moment she arrived so vividly. Swaddled in a cocoon of soft blankets, I could see how much it meant to her as dad pushed her wheelchair through the door. Though she was delicate and drained, there were smiles. I definitely saw smiles.

On Wednesday morning, the atmosphere at the school gate was stewing with tension and questions. From what I overheard, several parents were backing Mrs Bonson's proposal to reinstate Mr Blafferty.

"It won't happen! Will it?" A.J. asked, saddling up beside me. "They won't make her leave! Will they?"

I shrugged because that was all I could think to do - a weak and powerless shrug. How quickly everything had changed. It had only been two days, but my perspective on school had completely transformed. For months, I counted down the days, ticking them off in my mind the moment every SMARP exam ended but now I was longing for each day to linger - to last.

After a memorable Monday and a terrific Tuesday, a return to Blafferty's soul-sapping timetable would make minutes seem like months.

By the time we took our seats in the assembly hall, our hearts were brimming with hope.

Tap dancing animals? Check!

World Record Slam Dunks? Check!

"How could she possibly top those two?" Sebastian wondered as we sat waiting, desperate to rip the wrapping off Wednesday morning's surprise.

On the dot of nine, tiny footsteps echoed across the hall. A.J. squealed a little squeal as her brown curls shook with excitement. Instantly, the blue velvet curtains whipped back to reveal Mrs Mayhew standing on stage beside a paint-speckled easel.

Placed directly behind her, spread across the stage in a semi-circle, were twelve smaller easels. My eyes scanned the stage while my brain spun with wonder, desperate to figure out what was on today's menu. The half-moon of easels was broken in the centre by a large wooden square, the size of a garage door, made up of twelve shelves: four across, three down.

Dressed for another amazing day; Mrs Mayhew wore a pair of blue framed glasses upon a friendly but focused expression. Her brown shoes were held closed by blue-ribbon laces while twinkling sapphires buttoned her dove-white blouse. Just like Monday, just like Tuesday, she started with a song,

"May you always live your life,

let the right moment arrive.

May you always love your life,

in that moment, you will thrive."

A few tried to sing along, but because the second and fourth line were different yet again, they filled the gaps with mumbles and guesses. On the quick click of her fingers, Mr Paradisi toddled out carrying a paintbrush that looked like a giant spear within his titchy paws. A clutter of clapping and cheering rang out the instant her mini-assistant emerged. Revelling in the adulation, the cheeky fur-ball dithered in the middle of the stage and bowed. Another quick click of Mrs Mayhew's fingers was enough to remind her little friend of his objective.

While we looked on, Mrs Mayhew retrieved the brush and began to paint. Her shoulders shuffled. Her brown hair bounced. Her left hand sloshed and swished paint across the canvas. But few of us could see what she was actually doing.

"No chance this will top yesterday," Bradley predictably predicted while a handful of neighbouring allies nodded in agreement.

A sparrow-sized sigh fluttered from A.J.'s lips, "Looks like we might be out of magic."

Turning away from the easel, Mrs Mayhew revealed her painting. Nobody clapped. Faces were filled with "...so what?" expressions and everyone in the hall seemed a little underwhelmed.

Everyone - except me.

A wild shiver shuddered through me. My eyes were wide. My mouth was wide. Even my nostrils had expanded. It was a butterfly.

A Blue Morpho butterfly.

"Is it a coincidence?" part of me wondered, "but how could she know?" the other half reasoned.

Disinterested bodies began to budge as if the morning assembly was drawing to a close, but Mr Paradisi's sudden return halted the impending exodus. Carrying a small, golden lantern, he stood in the centre of the stage and on Mrs Mayhew's cue, pulled the lid of the lantern up and open.

One hundred and eighty-eight gaping gasps hoovered the air from the room as a colourful cloud of butterflies escaped the lantern. Fluttering and lolloping above our heads, flashes of yellow, orange and red created an enchanting kaleidoscope.

"One landed on me!" a little boy, three rows from the front, blurted before rising from his chair.

"Me too!" another cried, a few places to his right.

A smiling Mrs Mayhew beckoned the chosen students towards her with a gentle wave of her hand. Further through the crowd, the butterflies ventured, flapping their painted sails above our heads. As they landed upon their chosen human-runways, each student carefully stood up and walked gingerly towards the stage with their flutter-friend still attached.

"Red light! Red light!" Sebastian whispered loudly as a yellow spotted delight hovered near his head, "I don't like bugs!"

The most stunning, copper-winged Red Admiral wavered over Seb's cowering head and trimmed its flight to land directly on the knuckles of my left hand. Though I briefly twitched, the "flying flower" stayed put.

"She's waving you up Willow!" A.J. whispered while I sat transfixed by the delicate blades resting upon me.

As those sitting to my right nudged their knees out of my way and pushed their bags further under their chairs, I finally got the hint.

After I joined everyone on stage, Mrs Mayhew's soft clap summoned the butterflies to depart the hands and heads of the selected twelve and return to Mr Paradisi's open lantern. The tiny tap dancer scuttled from the stage but after a few seconds, he returned carrying a collection of paintbrushes that looked like a hastily stacked pile of firewood. As one tumbled from the bundle, he stumbled over it and spun forward, creating a fuzzy Ferris-wheel. Half the hall laughed while the rest "awwwwwd" in sympathy. Shaking himself off, Mr Paradisi quickly returned to his duties and armed us with our paintbrushes.

Waving her right arm and opening her palm, Mrs Mayhew was attempting to gesture something, but none of us were quite sure what. We knew we should paint - but what?

"What do you want us to paint, Miss?" a little girl with green eyes, three to my right, inquired.

Mrs Mayhew threw out her arms and

shrugged which to me (because I'm an expert in wordless communication) meant "whatever you like!" but my fellow painters were still stumped.

"Should we paint butterflies, Miss?" Tabitha Guild asked.

After clearing her throat, Mrs Mayhew slowly instructed, "Any ... any ... animal ... you ... wish."

Nobody else seemed to notice but I spotted something strange as she spoke. It was slow and laboured and she tapped the beat of each word upon her leg with her index finger. Despite my curiosity, I dared not ponder for longer because the others were already slapping their canvas with paint smothered brushes.

While my mother had enough talent to flood a giant's jacuzzi, I couldn't fill a fairy's egg cup. The Sylphina Angel briefly flashed across my eyes, but I knew I'd never do it justice.

Anyway, nothing was fresher in my mind than the dazzling Red Admiral that had just kissed my knuckles. With wild strokes, I gave it my all as the watching hundreds shuffled in their seats, craning to get a decent view of the menagerie of strange animals we were bringing to life.

Flicking my wrist with a final flourish, I was done. Stepping back, I suddenly realised that everyone was waiting for me. I was so absorbed in the challenge; I hadn't noticed.

After handing us small, slightly damp towels to wipe our spattered hands, Mrs Mayhew held her hands aloft and theatrically clapped in an attempt to coax the reluctant audience into applause. Taking our cue, we departed the stage.

As I took my seat, A.J. whispered a hearty, "Well done. It's beautiful." Instinctively, I assumed she was being kind although I soon noticed that, compared to the others, mine at least resembled some sort of animal.

"I can't specifically identify what number four is, but I do think it was hit by something at high speed," A.J. joked before her tone changed, "and I'm not sure what her plan is for these pictures, but right now, I think she should drag out the ol' basketball hoop."

A.J. was right. Now that I was back amongst the crowd, I could feel the restless energy simmering around me. Monday's and Tuesday's assemblies had been occasions that we would remember forever. Edge of the seat stuff that made clocks flash forward and hearts flutter. But Wednesday's was all a bit drawn out. (Pardon the pun)

"I think I'm ready to sign that petition!" Bradley teased, spurring a handful around him to giggle.

After gathering up our paintings, Mrs Mayhew placed them within the individual squares of the frame assembled in the centre of the stage.

"I think she's creating a mosaic," Sebastian commented before he spotted some crumpled expressions around him, "it's one big picture made up of smaller ones," he clarified.

With the twelve paintings now housed in separate windows, Mrs Mayhew began rotating them, trying to make something out of the mess of swirls, spots and blotches. So far, they weren't adding up to anything even remotely recognisable.

"If you squint, it looks a bit like a … nappy exploding!" Bradley jested while A.J. sighed at the sight of our hero struggling so much. I too was fretting; my palms were oiling up while my right leg gyrated.

I was sure that we were scarcely moments away from an audible BOOOO! or the chanting of Blafferty's name. A buzz of hardly hidden whispers was already swarming around the hall.

"Look!" A.J. cried before squeezing my leg, "something's happening."

Somehow, as she continued to spin and swap the square canvases, a shape was forming. The whispers were slowly fading. Heads swivelled back towards the stage. The twelve random animals (including something hit by a car and my Red Admiral) were taking a new form - a new shape - like a caterpillar breaking from its cocoon, ready to spread its crisp, new wings.

"It's a butterfly!" several voices echoed together the instant she spun the canvas in the top right corner.

"Nah, can't see it!" Bradley moaned. "Still looks like a nappy bomb!"

Though not quite the masterpiece she had created ten minutes earlier, I could see something. My painting, turned on its side, made up half of the right wing while the right ear of Tabitha's elephant made up the rest. The legs of somebody's orange (yes orange!) flamingo had been spun around to look like the antennae. With her mosaic complete, the picture spinner stood to one side to a smatter of mild applause.

"It took a while, but that's pretty decent," A.J. admitted, "although I don't think it's exciting enough to make the evening news."

But Mrs Mayhew wasn't done.

She was building towards something.

Suddenly, she clapped - a sharp, echoey clap that filled the hall.

The painting moved.

The large, painted wings twitched.

"Did that just move?" Sebastian questioned, shooting up out of his chair.

Mrs Mayhew didn't answer his very public inquiry. Instead she clapped again. Louder. Faster. More intense. Once more, the wings twitched. Quicker than before, as if the paint briefly lifted from the canvas then suddenly returned.

"It's a demon!" Sebastian groaned.

She clapped again. Three quick claps that made all the paint depart the canvas. Right before our eyes, the wild splashes of a dozen different animals re-arranged to look like one mega-butterfly somehow transformed into a colourful canopy as hundreds of butterflies fluttered above our heads. The front rows squealed with delight as they pushed their open hands into the air and let the flock flicker through their fingers. Giggles filled giddy throats as the silken rainbow swooped across the hall, pulsing and bathing within the crowd below.

Tickling our faces.

Kissing our hands.

A soft, speedy rustling, sounding like the wind whispering secrets, filled our ears. Sebastian wasn't quite so enthralled; crouching down with his head between his knees, he looked like he was on a plane about to crash land into the sea.

"This is what heaven feels like," A.J. yelped while waving her hands amongst the fluttering rush.

Butterflies of every colour gloved my hands while the most beautiful zebra-striped Swallowtail rested upon the tip of my nose, tickling me with its twitching antennae.

Suddenly, a thunderously loud clap summoned the hovering kaleidoscope back towards the stage. To our utter amazement, the crazy canopy waltzed and flickered against the blank canvas but they did not bounce back. Somehow, they blended back in to recreate the mega-butterfly made from our twelve random animals.

Though A.J. and I were first to stand, it didn't take long for those seated nearby to join us. Whooping like chimps, we flapped our wings and clapped our hands, overjoyed by whatever it was we had just witnessed. I had no idea if it was magic or madness but I was truly spellbound. My eyes, mouth and nostrils were wider than ever before.

"I saw some guy do that on Britain's Got Talent!" sniped Bradley who stubbornly remained anchored to his chair along with Jarvis Bonson and one or two others. "She just switched the picture when we stopped looking because we were so bored."

"But how do you explain how they went back into the picture?" A.J. rallied back, fed up with his tiresome whinging.

"When they fly all around it, someone behind switches the paintings around again," he shouted over the applause.

Know-It-All-Boy might have stopped looking, but I never took my eyes off her. Not once. Not even for a split-second. As the ovation finally faded and we took our seats, A.J. noticed something else,

"Willow, you're crying!" she declared louder than expected.

"That was so amazing," I announced as everybody nearby turned towards me in startled surprise.

11

Signal Loss

Tears flushed my face, but my throat was drier than dust.

"You just spoke!" A.J. beamed with a smile that didn't reflect my mood.

While I should have hugged or high-fived her, all I could think to do was run. Trundling through a blockade of knees and tuts, I dragged my bag like a reluctant infant. As I broke free of my row, Mrs Mayhew's voice echoed in the air behind me,

> "May you always live your life,
>   let the right moment arrive.
> May you always love your life,
>   in that moment you will thrive."

A loud sob cracked across the empty

playground as the cold air hit my face.

"Willow! Willow!" Mrs Murphy's faint voice followed behind.

But there was only one voice I wanted to hear. Needing silence and a door with a lock, I set my satnav for the girl's toilets and floored it. My hair, bag and skirt struggled to keep pace as I hurried into the wind and crossed the playground. Though I could think of a thousand sanctuaries a million times more hygienic, I had no choice. Locking myself in the very last cubicle, I fumbled around in my bag, searching for my headphones.

"Sshh! Sshh!" I whispered, struggling to soothe my panicked breath and frantic mind as I flopped down upon the closed toilet seat.

"Please be there! Please be there!" I groaned while my trembling hands wrapped my headphones around my head.

Nothing.

Silence.

Cupping my hands around the soft, black leather, I tried to create a thicker coat of quiet. But nothing came, nothing except my own heavy breathing dulled to sound like it was in the next room. Then came the knocking: a distant but incessant knocking of knuckles on cheap, laminate wood.

In addition to drumming on the toilet door, Mrs Murphy was also firing a flurry of questions, but none of them were hitting the target. My headphones reduced her to a hazy echo while I tried to figure out how I could resurrect mum's voice and resuscitate her song; the song that looped around my head for three years.

"What if I sing it?" I wondered in the hope that it might somehow restart the melody.

"May you always live your-" I sang aloud before suddenly halting in disbelief.

The knocking grew louder: both in my heart and at the door.

"How could you forget the words?" I

whispered angrily before scrunching my hands into fists and digging my fingernails into my clammy palm. Not only could I no longer hear mum singing, now I was struggling to remember the lines of her lullaby. In its place, Mrs Mayhew's assembly song was rocketing around my mind, waiting to launch from my tongue.

Finally, Mum's words came tumbling,

"When you say goodnight,"

They were slow, but they were coming. Standing statue-still, I held my breath in the hope that mum would pick up the tune and sing the rest. But nothing came. Just more knocking. I had to keep trying.

"Know that I'm not far."

I paused.

Still nothing. Nothing except Mrs. Murphy knocking and knocking and knocking until I finally snapped. Like an over-inflated balloon that just went pop, in one move, I stood up, unlocked the door of the cubicle, whipped it back and stared directly into the slightly startled face of Mrs Murphy,

"Stop knocking! Stop knocking! STOP KNOCKING!" I screamed, "I'm trying to hear my mum's SONG!"

The word "SONG" was so loud and so long that it shuddered through me and did cruel things to her face. The sight of her stunned eyes and creased lips should have made me feel rotten, but it was a scene I couldn't register at the time. Explanations and apologies would come later - after mum's voice had come home. Hastily slamming the swinging panel shut, I sat down and began again,

"When you say goodnight,
know that I'm not far.
Lift your head up high,
I'm in between those stars."

I fell quiet and waited, so sure her voice would find me. Yet the stubborn silence stayed. The shadow of rubber shoe soles between the floor and the door warned me that someone else had joined Mrs Murphy. Although the knocking had stopped, I knew they were listening -

listening to a strange girl sing in a toilet: a frustrated, tear-stained girl.

I tried the second verse,

> "If you need me don't you fret,
> I'll be with you day and night.
> Just lift your weary head,
> I'm in between starlight."

As soon as I stopped singing, a heavy, choking silence clung to me. I sobbed. Loud, uncontrollable sobs that sent snot sledding down my nostrils and bridged my lips with threads of spit. I kicked the cubicle door. I punched the cubicle wall. I picked up my bag and launched it towards the wall as if I was going for gold in the shot-put.

Pulling my headphones from my ears, I was just about to smash them against the door when a soft voice arrived,

"Willow?"

While it wasn't the voice I wanted, it was the voice I needed.

"Willow ... it's ... it's me ... Mrs Mayhew.

Please … let me … talk to… you," she asked.

Her slow words and gentle voice were so soothing; they neutralised my frenzy.

Slowly, I pulled the slide-lock back.

12

The Perfect Snowball

"You have ... the ... loveliest ... voice." Mrs Mayhew remarked while gently tapping her hand on the polished, mahogany wood of her oddly presidential desk.

I had sat in front of enough head-teachers to know that this was not how a *normal* principal furnished their office. Not unless they worked as part-time teacher, part-time RULER OF THE WORLD. A lavish lamp, leather-bound books and a shining collection of canes nesting in one corner told me that this regal office was not by Mrs Mayhew's design: these were the grand fittings of a Blafferty.

"Is it ... your... your mum's song?" she asked from a black leather chair that she would never grow into.

Though I failed to reply immediately, a gentle nod and her lingering stare lulled me into an eventual nod of my own. Crumpling the soggy tissue she'd offered as I entered her office, I dabbed it beneath my eyes once more.

"It's a ... beautiful ... song," she appraised while softly drumming the tips of her left hand upon the desk in time with each word.

Lost in thought, I stared so intently at her rhythmic fingers that she blushed and repositioned her hand upon her lap. Although now hidden from view, I knew she was still tapping from the subtle twitch of her upper arm.

"Is she nervous about talking to me?" I wondered, "or maybe she's worried about the petition?"

"I ... I've read ... your file," she revealed with a sympathetic smile.

Immediately, I expected the predictable trio of, "I'm sorry for your loss," "it must have been tough" and "if I can help in any way" that everyone always spouted. But _she_ didn't.

"Have you ... ever ... ever had a ... snowball fight?" she unexpectedly inquired as I wiped the tears that refused to fade.

I was so taken aback by her strange query that it took me a moment to recall if I ever had. Eventually, a hazy memory ebbed into my mind of mum waltzing my four-year-old self through the air in a snow blanketed park. Mrs Mayhew must have known I was busy re-stitching the memory because she let the silence settle around us without urging a response. Finally, I smiled and nodded, prompting her to share her recollection,

"When I was ... a little ... younger than you ... the biggest ... whitest snowfall ... I had ... ever seen ... fell all around ... my ... my house. The second ... we ... woke up ... we all ran down ... downstairs ... in our pyjamas ... and rushed straight outside. There were five ... of us ... my ... my two brothers ... two sisters ... and me. I was the youngest. My brothers were ... going crazy grabbing handfuls ... and throwing the biggest ....

snowballs as hard as ... they could ... while my two ... my two sisters ... pinched ... little fingerfuls and ... threw them in the air ... and most of it ... blew back ... on them ... falling into their open eyes ... and laughing mouths ... but I stood there ... with this most ... perfect snowball ... in my hand. I had rolled it ... around so much ... it was so ... perfectly smooth ... perfectly round. And because I could not ... bare to lose it ... I didn't dare throw it. Instead I ... I went back inside ... into our living room and ... sat upon my father's ... favourite armchair."

Her story was so mesmerising, I didn't realise how much my nose was running. With a subtle lift of her eyebrows and a delicate tap of her nose, she prompted me to use my tissue.

On she spoke. On she tapped, "... upon his chair ... I cradled my snowball .... rolling it gently ... between ... my hands. Because I loved ... how smooth it felt ... I decided ... that I was going to ... to keep it forever. I even ... gave it a name. But of course ... because the room ... was so warm and...

because my hands ... could not stop ... touching it ... my little white friend ... began to melt. After just a ... few minutes ... my hands ... were dripping wet ... and the top of my ... pyjama legs ... where my arms ... were resting ... were drenched."

I laughed aloud; a little laugh that started like a sob but ended with a chuckle. My sob-laugh appeared to momentarily worry Mrs Mayhew before she realised I was fine and matched my giggle,

"... and I don't ... know why ... but instead of running ... back outside ... and rolling it ... in a new layer of snow ... I ... I grasped it even tighter ... because in my head...I was so convinced... that if I held on ... as tightly as I could ... it could never ... ever leave. But ... of course ... the more I tried ... holding on to it ... the faster it melted. I was ba- ... I was basically ... crushing it ....and before long ... it disappeared ... right through my fingers ... and to add ... to my sorrow ... my father came downstairs ... to find his ... favourite chair

... dripping with melted snow ... he was so angry ... he banished me ... to my room ... for the rest ... of the day ... where I sat ... by my window ... watching my brothers ... and sisters ... enjoy a day of fun ... in the snow."

The drumming paused as her lips froze. The painful memory of the punishment lingered in the air between us for a second before she cleared her throat and continued,

"Willow ... the more you ... try to hold on ... to your mum's song ... the more you try ... to protect it ... the more it will ... slip ... slip through your fingers. Look ... at that tissue ... in your hand ... which you've been ... twisting and squeezing. It's no good ... anymore ... is it?" she asked while holding out the box to offer another.

"I promise that ... if ... if you let go ... of that song ... if you stop ... fearing you ... might forget it ... I promise you ... it will return. Another song ... or melody ... might come along ... and take its place ... but that won't stay ... either. Trust me ... tonight or maybe ... tomorrow night or maybe some morning ... next week ... when you're brush ... brushing your teeth ... her voice will ... come back. I'm sure ... your ... your mum ... wouldn't want ... you working so ... so hard to ... keep her voice alive ... that you ... risk losing ... your own."

It was then that the second tissue got it. All of it.

Floods of tears.

Waves of sobs.

Mrs Mayhew waited patiently for it to pass before asking,

"Could ... you help ... me with ... tomorrow's assembly. It's going to be ... all about music ... and at ... lunchtime today, I'm ... I'm going to ... rehearse ... with the junior .... classes in the ... assembly hall. I don't ... think you ... play an instrument ... but I hoped ... you might sing ... just a line."

My outsides shrugged while my insides shook. I had spoken no more than five words in three years so how was I supposed to sing (ON

STAGE!) in front of everyone? Despite the gnawing feeling that I couldn't let her down, I also couldn't bring myself to commit.

"Will you please ... think about it?" she asked before handing me a thin strip of paper with the words of Thursday's song printed upon it. I nodded. It was the least I could do.

By the time I dried my eyes and waited for the red blotches to fade, everyone in Year 6 was armed with brushes and covered in paint.

Despite slipping in as nonchalantly as I could, A.J. quickly hunted me down. Wiping her paint-stained hands upon her apron, she checked if I was okay before rapidly relaying the instructions for the morning session,

"We're making a mural, and Mrs Murphy says we can paint two or three of our favourite things, like a person we love, a place we've been to or an object we can't live without. I'm painting an ice-cream and a Big-Mac cause I'm hoping Mrs Mayhew comes in and does her magic clappy thing that makes them come alive," she joked.

Despite my mournful morning, the thought of A.J. standing by the wall waiting for her Frankenstein burger to come to life almost made me laugh. Most of the class were already half-way through painting Netflix, Xbox or McDonald's logos in strange, new colours while a few managed to summon up enough emotion to paint love hearts, puppy dogs and stick-men families holding hands.

"I've saved you a little corner near the bottom Willow," Mrs Murphy informed me after spotting my return, "good to have you back."

Reflecting my mood, I decided to paint my square black. Nothing inside it. Just a big black box. The moment she spied it, poor Mrs Murphy looked somewhat concerned,

"You are allowed to use more than one colour, Willow," she advised.

Once it was dry, I stitched three shimmering stars into my jet black box with egg-yolk yellow paint. Around the stars, I dabbed angel white blotches to recreate the snowstorm of Mrs Mayhew's memory. Beneath the snow and below the stars, I added two cupped hands: empty hands aching to hold something or someone.

13

Hippo Heavy

I didn't make it to rehearsals.

Mrs Murphy was so impressed with our mural she wondered, "would anyone like to stay for lunch to help me smother my other wall in butterflies? I've got custard creams!"

I sprung my hand up into the air so swiftly that my arm nearly launched from its socket. 51% of my willingness to assist Mrs Murphy came from my love of butterflies and memories of mum while 45% came from a throat-swelling, eye-popping fear of ever having to sing or talk or even whisper in front of a crowd. (In case you're wondering, the remaining 4% was due to the custard creams ☺)

Wednesday should have been a tonne of

fun as each year group rotated around different workshops, exploring the curious and colourful world of art but nothing could lift my mood. Though it had been three years since mum passed, she never felt far away. But without her song, everywhere was quieter. Everything was heavier. Each time I moved, it felt like I was dragging a suitcase filled with a family of hippos. Even wriggling my toes took effort.

As soon as I found a moment to slip away, I snuck back into the toilet cubicle, still determined to retune my brain to her radio frequency. Though I tried the headphones; though I revved the song; though I stuffed my ear nostrils with cheap, itchy tissue paper, the only thing I heard was teachers moaning every time I turned up late and missed the introduction to their workshop.

Those hippos were getting heavier.

Mrs Mayhew had organised everything from recreating cave paintings with chisels to portrait-painting of Mr Paradisi saluting the sky in a super-tiny, super-cute sailors' uniform. After lunch, Year 6 ended the day with a pop art masterclass where we painted sweets, soup cans, zebras and a few other everyday items in vibrant and unexpected colours. My jet-black lollipop topped with razor-sharp spikes didn't quite match the rainbow creations that freshened up the cracked classroom walls.

"Do you like my purple dog with six legs?" A.J. asked, trying to lighten my mood. "These two legs on top, I know they look like wings, but they are actually extra paws so he can reach around and scratch his own belly and doesn't have to keep hinting at his owners!"

The hippos slimmed as a reluctant laugh fell from my mouth.

"It's so kind of your baby brother to drop by and paint that dog!" a lingering Jarvis Bonson japed, creating another tidal wave of scornful laughter.

"I will pass on your kind wishes Jarvis," A.J. calmly replied without turning to face him.

"Sorry if I've interrupted your conversation?" he jested. "Oh sorry! I forgot your only friend doesn't talk."

The hippos were swelling again. By this point, my day was already so bad, I felt like I had absolutely nothing to lose. Shoving this clown over and humiliating him in front of his sniggering chums would be well worth any potential punishment coming my way. But A.J.'s failure to rise to the bait calmed my rage. Ignoring his petty barbs, she continued to stare straight ahead while talking to me, "it's a shame that black lollipop of yours isn't real. It could be very useful."

Although it was likely that Jarvis was very familiar with being ignored, he refused to take the hint as he was determined to get a reaction,

"I can see where Willow gets her inspiration. That lollipop looks ... quite like you," he swiped with a wobbly smile although the last three words seemed reluctant to leave his mouth. They were laboured and slow. As were his friends who knew he'd crossed the line.

I certainly wasn't laughing - because I was too busy launching myself towards him. My rage was instinctive and my finger nails were sharp. But before I could get near the swine's smug and smiling face, A.J. caught me by my flailing left arm and hauled me back.

I assumed she was restraining me because she had her own master plan for physical, or at least verbal, revenge. Yet as the snivelling, floppy-haired bully stood there anticipating the bite back, A.J. didn't even take a nip. Keeping her back turned to him, she hid the small tears welling up in the corner of each eye and bowed her head.

"Enjoy your final days of painting and dancing 'cause my mother's going to make sure Blafferty's back by Monday," Jarvis jeered before scuttling off.

A.J. sighed like a cracked gas pipe.

"Why didn't you do something?" I blurted in frustration.

She didn't reply. Shaking her head, she pursed her lips and gazed unblinkingly at the discoloured linoleum floor.

"Or why didn't you let me?" I probed while crouching my knees in an attempt to catch her eye.

"I need you here," she finally replied, each word sagging with the weight of her sadness, "if you touch him, you'll get expelled."

"But the school would have understood, and he would have been the one getting in trouble for what he said," I pleaded.

She didn't respond but coughed a half sob, half-chuckle.

"What's so funny?" I pecked in exasperation.

"He's untouchable," she scoffed, "like my mum always says - 'those who have the gold make the rules' and trust me, with Jarvis, she's right!"

Shortly after 3.15, A.J. drowsily shook a shoe box full of tickets in front of a fingers-crossed crowd who had gathered by the school gate. Mrs Mayhew glowed with a warm smile as she gladly drew a winning ticket from a scissor-cut slot (barely big enough for her hand – OOPS!). After retrieving the ticket (and her hand), she passed it to A.J. who announced in a flat, disinterested tone,

"One-eight-eight. Anyone? Number ONE! EIGH! EIGHT!"

Briefly, I thought I had won because the number was the same as the ranking rectangle I stood within on my first day at Thrive Academy until I remembered that I'd forgotten to enter.

"Anyone … ONE! EIGHT! EIGHT!" A.J. impatiently repeated while people ruffled through handbags and turned out pockets.

"That's mine! That's mine!" a triumphant voice crowed from somewhere inside the crush.

"Isn't this wonderful," A.J. declared through gritted, sarcastic teeth, "the lucky lady with the winning ticket is none other than Mrs Bonson."

"Where is my prize?" the cake winner rudely inquired without a hint of gratitude, "I expect you will deliver it to my house as soon as possible."

14

(HEART) BREAKING NEWS

The minute I returned to STINKIN' SCREAMIN' RUBBISH HOLE, I flew straight towards my nest. After pulling the curtains shut, I climbed under my duvet without even bothering to remove my Dismal Air uniform. Once the chattering springs in my "antique" mattress settled, I prayed the silence might allow mum's song to return.

Nothing.

The more I forced it; the more my frustration swelled until loud sobs filled the self-made cave I'd engineered around my head. After an hour of trying and waiting and nothing, dad arrived through the door and shouted from the bottom of the stairs, "Chicken pesto pasta with garlic dough balls ready in thirty minutes!"

I had no appetite. None whatsoever.

Not hungry! bad headake! I text as the meagre glow of my phone's screen guided my fingers through the dark.

R u sure! Its 1 of ur faves ☺, he text back.

Not wanting to be rude, I popped down half an hour later to smile hello and kiss him goodnight. Despite looking slightly concerned for my welfare, dad was also super delighted that he no longer had to divvy up the dough balls. As I leaned over his favourite armchair to kiss him goodnight, the television spat a familiar voice into my ears.

"... and finally this evening, our education correspondent couldn't leave Ickleton without fully investigating strange reports of dancing monkeys at Thrive Academy. Emily, what can you tell us?"

As the dim drizzle fell around her, Emily Nouveaux's brown eyes buzzed with anticipation.

"Well, Eileen, I can tell you that I stand outside the gates of a school that boasts a very special and slightly strange head-teacher. Not only did Mrs Mayhew break that slam-dunk world record yesterday but on Monday, she tap-danced with her pet meerkat, and only moments ago, I learned that, during this morning's assembly, she somehow made hundreds of butterflies fly out of a painting."

Dad spun his neck towards me with his eyebrows elevated as if to say, "You never said." (Or "You never text" in our situation.) I jiggled three quick nods which was the internationally agreed body language code for, "yes, it happened."

Miss Reporter hadn't finished reporting, "But, unfortunately, Mrs Mayhew may not have many assemblies left because the petition to reinstate the suspended principal, Mr Blafferty, has attracted over two hundred signatures. As a result, Thrive Academy's chair of governors, Mrs Deehan has released a statement confirming that this Friday, they will hold a meeting with all members of the governing body in Ickleton Village Hall to discuss the current situation and vote on Mr Blafferty's potential return."

Vaulting off the side of dad's chair, I growled at the TV, "The only thing that clown should return is the six months of my life he stole with his stinkin' tests and stinkin' books and stinkin' assemblies!"

Dad got such a fright, he jolted upright in his recliner, spilling his dough balls across the carpet. My heart pounded within my chest as Jarvis' chilling threat rang like a doomsday siren through my ears. Mr Blafferty could return. Ranking rectangles could be resurrected.

In full-moon surprise, Dad's eyes stared towards me, but I didn't have time to explain; the reporter was still reporting, and now clutching a white piece of paper in her hand. Grabbing the remote, I turned up the volume,

"This afternoon, we received a statement from Mr Blafferty thanking the community of

Ickleton for their support. It reads, "How can I ever repay the loyalty shown by the people of Ickleton? My faithful parents and students, these outrageous accusations are nothing but fake, fraudulent news dreamed up by the treacherous media who wish to tear me down. I will show everyone during Friday's inquiry that this is the greatest hoax in history. I wish to thank Mrs Mayhew for doing a sterling job keeping things ticking over in my absence but my students need a head-teacher who is bringing the future of education into the present, not a supply teacher who's stuck in the past."

"Supply teacher?" I roared. "I'll supply you with a five-knuckle sandwich you ungrateful pig!" I screamed again while dad blew carpet hair from his recaptured dough balls.

"Whoa! Whoa! Whoa! Easy there, Tiger. What's got you so worked up?" dad soothed.

"He has to be sacked!" I raged with a face unfit for photographs, "HE'S A RAT!!"

"Take it easy mouse. We don't even know

what he's been accused of," dad reasoned before surrendering his half-full bowl to the coffee table.

"He's a rat," I echoed again in sad, wobbly sounds.

Wrapping his arms around me, dad dished out one of his trademark squeezy hugs which always made me feel, for the few seconds they lasted, invincible from everything.

"And when may I ask about the sudden return of your voice?" he wondered.

Twenty-one text messages were enough to explain the day. He'd likely hoped I'd actually tell him, but the moment my rage subsided, my mouth dried up again. I feared that if I got stuck in a lengthy back and forth (or a *conversation* as normal people call it) that I'd have no chance of relocating mum.

Sleep was hard to find.

While the clock claimed it had been only two hours and seventeen minutes, I felt like I'd been twisting, turning and turning and twisting for seventeen eternities. For so long, I had mum's angelic voice to sing me to sleep but, in the silence, I felt lost. Finally, I gave in and got up.

Switching my jelly bean lamp on, I slumped into my writing desk and flicked open my laptop. Willow Hushley's five-step plan for a perfect life had taken a backseat since Mrs Mayhew arrived. *Surfing on Starlight* had been ignored for almost a week. I was too busy trying to fix the present to worry about shaping my future.

I typed *HELP MAYHEW HELP MAYHEW HELP MAYHEW HELP MAYHEW HELP MAYHEW* across the screen over and over until it was pure gibberish, *HELP PAYMEW PLEH WEHYAM HELP HELP HELP PLEH PLEH PLEH*.

Just before my twitching fingers halted upon the keyboard, one possible resolution popped into my mind, *DESTROY BLAFFERTY DESTROY BLAFFERTY DESTROY BLAFFERTY*.

It was then that I figured it out. Mrs Mayhew didn't need my help; she was exactly where I needed her to be. All I had to do was make sure Blafferty never set foot in my school again.

But how?

Scratching around my tired and aching brain, I searched for something, anything that might keep Blafferty at bay. I even typed "how to destroy Mr Blafferty" into Google, but Google didn't understand; *"Did you mean:* **how to destroy a filthy lavatory***?"*

Friday evening's meeting would decide his future, my future and the future of any child who might ever set foot in Thrive Academy. If only I could somehow sneak into the meeting to do or say something that would make the governors see him through my eyes - not how the golden tie brigade and all their precious parents did. The way I did. The way A.J. did. The way every single child who was treated like a number and left to rot in the never-ending oblivion that lay between the top ten and the bottom ten did.

But how was I, a girl who can't even talk to her dad, supposed to sneak into a meeting she's not invited to, stand up in front of a group of strangers and convince them that they are all idiots who are falling for the biggest pack of lies? No matter how hard I tried, nothing was coming. No clues. No sparks. No ideas. Eventually, sleep snuck up on me.

A few hours later, I awoke at my desk. The room was cold and quiet, but something was stirring. Something at the back of my ear. A faint but familiar sound. Grabbing my headphones, I wrapped them around my ears and stood deathly still. Mrs Mayhew had suggested mum's song would return when I least expected it, but as I held my breath to hush my breathing, I realised that it wasn't mum's voice. Nor was it her song.

"May you always live your life!"

Mrs Mayhew's assembly song was whirring through my head,

"May you soar to greater heights!"

I half expected to fly into a fit of rage. To panic. To kick. To scream. To wake dad up at four in the morning. I didn't. Instead I slowly breathed out one super-long breath and reminded myself of Mrs Mayhew's advice: mum's voice would return.

As my arm brushed against the laptop, the screen lit up and reminded me of my plan to DESTROY BLAFFERTY, and while I wasn't yet sure how I could achieve it, I knew exactly how to help Mrs Mayhew.

I had to sing for her.

15

Musical Mayhem

"**A**nd love everything you do," was the line Mrs Mayhew wanted me to sing.

Over and over again, I rehearsed those five words until the sun squeaked through my curtains at 6.30.

"Morning songbird!" dad chirped as he popped his head around my door, "Best alarm clock ever!"

"Mrs Mayhew wants me to sing in today's assembly!" I burst, in the first proper sentence I'd spoken to my father in years.

"Wow," he replied while flicking his pillow-beaten hair with his fingers, "you sure you're ready for it mouse?"

"AND LOVE EVERY - THING YOU DO!" I sang my reply.

"You are! So, does this mean we can replace the kitchen radio?" he asked beneath a cheeky grin.

"Not yet," I said, smiling back.

Arriving at the school gate just after 8.30, I immediately felt the absence of one beautiful bunch of brown curls. Despite scanning every face twice over, I couldn't find A.J. In the six months I had known her, she'd never missed a single day and always beat me to the school gate, but now I feared the worst; Jarvis and his jokers had become too much for her.

Everyone waiting was in hyper-chatty, super-gossip mode; prattling and tattling about last night's news. The big-gobs were already calling the result of Friday's vote,

"Blafferty's back on Monday so we might actually learn something," Charles cheeped.

"I'm so glad tomorrow's her last day, I really can't stand that stupid song," Barnaby beeped.

"It will be a landslide. Only the babies in

year one will miss her," Simon squeaked.

I longed to have the confidence to find the right words to knock them out with a witty, clever repost but nothing came tumbling. Instead, I eyeballed every one of them with really pointy, dagger stares which I held firm until Bradley furnished us with his latest conspiracy theory.

"Even if she was allowed to, I don't think she'll stand up for herself at the meeting," he blurted just before the blue gates opened to signal the start of our morning march.

"Why wouldn't she?" Sebastian asked.

"She can't talk," Bradley snarked through a slithering, know-it-all smile.

"Of course, she can talk, she's delivered three assemblies!" Sebastian replied with an impatient guffaw.

"She might have done three assemblies but she's hardly spoken a single word. You watch her today. I swear on my pet rat's life, there's something up with that supply teacher!" he avowed while making the sign of an X with his right index finger across his chest.

"You're such an idiot!" I spat much to everyone's surprise, "She sings in every assembly and she's spoken to me twice!"

"Well, you're hardly an expert on the art of talking," Jarvis Bonson suddenly chipped in as his team of spineless shadows giggled behind him.

Despite trying to resist their provocation, my mouth moved without my brain's invitation, "Just because you can talk, doesn't mean you've got anything worth listening to."

Silence fell and eyebrows wrinkled, as my unexpected counter-punch appeared to fly over everyone's befuddled heads. Bradley was determined to have the final word on the matter.

"She might not be a mute but other than a few words, she's said nothing. You watch today's assembly, I bet my Xbox controllers she won't say a single word!" Bradley predicted with confidence.

"I wouldn't blame her if she never came back here at all," Sebastian cried with a sigh that made a sudden and unexpected fear rise within me. Seb had a point. Why would Mrs Mayhew stay when two hundred signatures made it crystal clear they wanted her out?

As we took our seats, the plastic chair to my left was so cold and so empty, I genuinely feared A.J. might soon have to survive *her* first day at a new school. Before any more gossiping or guessing could begin, the royal blue curtains retreated to reveal an assembly hall stage that was the opposite of empty. Bursting with shining silver and glimmering brass, it twinkled and flickered like Aladdin's cave of wonders.

A set of drums, two harps, a tandem of trumpets, a couple of cellos, a bundle of bass guitars, a pair of pianos, a glut of electric guitars and a duo of double bass sat sternly on the stage.

"Red light! Red light!" Sebastian groaned, rocking back and forth a little.

"What's wrong?" I whispered.

"I don't like loud noises," he gulped.

Reaching into my bag, I plucked out my headphones, "Try these Seb. You'll still be able to hear it, but they turn the volume right down," I explained as he gratefully grabbed them from my outstretched hand.

Cowering before this fierce parade of instruments sat a conductor's podium. A little baton leaned upon it as if awaiting the arrival of its musical master. Although, Mrs Mayhew was nowhere to be seen.

"Why are there so many empty seats?" I wondered aloud though A.J.'s empty chair and Seb's head-phoned ears couldn't hear me. Unfortunately, Bradley Bogstein could.

"That's the Mayhew effect - three days in and they're already looking for a new school," he announced, breaking yet another "fake-news" story.

Without warning, Mr Paradisi scuttled from the wings. Wearing a little, black bow-tie and tailcoat, he scampered up the podium to claim the miniature baton as his. Flicking a quick double tap, he signalled the entrance of a large group of students who lumbered out of the shadows. Walking two-by-two, they looked somewhat rattled beneath the bright, blinding lights.

Two halted by the harps.

Two sat ready to rock behind the drums.

Two bore the weight of the gigantic cellos.

Two set their fingers upon their pianos.

Two got ready to jangle on electric guitars.

Two tweaked and tuned their double bass.

Two locked their lips upon the trumpets.

Two perched their fingers on their bass guitar strings.

A half-inflated balloon of hope that A.J. might walk out with the band quickly popped when I realised the orchestra was made up entirely of Year 1 students. Another tap of his tiny twig instantly summoned a secret second group who shot up out of the sitting crowd like a pod of dolphins jumping from the sea.

Bouncing across the stage, this mix of all ages hastily created parallel rows with the slightly taller students standing behind. Right before they settled into position, the back row shifted an inch to the right so their smiling faces were nestled between the shoulders of those standing in front.

Yet, something seemed wrong. Everything so far had even numbers but the front row of the choir had seven, and the back row had six. Someone was missing. Suddenly, the furry conductor, wearing a disgruntled expression upon his little face, swivelled back towards the crowd and pointed his baby branch directly towards me.

"Oops!" I gasped the instant I realised that it was, in fact, ME who was missing from the back row. Shuffling past knees and bags, I made my way up to the stage while frantically trying to remember the line I'd rehearsed all morning.

As I finally took my place in line, Mr Paradisi winked and flicked his tiny paws out of the sleeves of his jacket. Like a wizard about to enact his most daring spell, the meerkat checked his surrounding and tapped his musical wand seven times. The taps went LOUD, soft, LOUD, soft and got bigger and bigger as they proceeded. He was setting the rhythm for the mini musicians to follow his lead. The drummers slammed out a beat,

Bam! Bam! Bam! Bam!

Bam! Bam!

Bam!

Everyone sitting and standing instantly recognised the rhythm. Flicking his baton to the right, Mr Paradisi then triggered the choir to burst into song.

May you always

live your

life!

The same six words and seven syllables that opened Mrs Mayhew's morning assembly now had a booming backing track. Without warning, Mr Paradisi stretched out his paws and signalled to the drummers and EVERY member of the choir to join in,

May you al-ways

live your

life!

Bam!

Bam! Bam!

Bam! Bam! Bam! Bam!

Before another note arrived, Mr Paradisi spun 180 degrees to face the smiling crowd. As he raised his petit-paws into the air, a light dusting of steps echoed from the back of the hall. Appearing above the seated, swivelling heads bobbed a very familiar flock of digestive coloured hair.

Although she really was a tiny teacher, her grand entrance assured me of one thing; Mrs Mayhew was not about to wave the white flag. As she climbed the four steps to the stage, her long, yellow skirt swished below her knees like a golden flag. Yellow ribbons adorned her slip-on shoes while a chain of butter-yellow beads hung snug around her neck. Little black splashes dotted her honey spectacles. After passing the baton, Mr Paradisi was greeted with the gentlest pat on the head before he scurried over to join the two tots on drums. Raising the melody-maker, Mrs Mayhew turned and bowed to the waiting crowd. At that very moment, I could see exactly who was with her and who wasn't. The majority of faces lit up with wide, yearning grins while the belligerent handful who still craved golden ties and unending tests sneered through narrow eyes. Wearing matching sunglasses, the two bass players positioned their fingers touch-tight upon the thick strings and plucked out a fat and wonderful sound,

Wump! Wamp! Wump! Wamp!

Wump! Wamp!

Wump!

Swiftly turning to the audience, Mrs Mayhew swooshed her arms into the air to invite the supportive majority to roar from the top of their lungs,

May you al-ways

live your

life!

Now it was over to the pianists who donked their digits on black and white keys the instant Mrs Mayhew whipped back around and pointed in their direction;

Clong-Clung! Clong-Clung!

Clong! Clung!

Clong!

This time, Mrs Mayhew didn't turn back to the audience. Whizzing to her left, she pointed towards Tabitha Guild sitting at the edge of the back row. The instant Tabby opened her little mouth, a massive voice fell out,

Ev – ery – day – try–

some – thing –

new!

With a whisk to the right, the crazed banana coloured lady pierced the air with her black needle while the guitarists sprang into action by fidgeting their fingers along the strings,

Twing! Twang! Twang! Twing!

Twang! Twing!

Twang!

The final twang had hardly twung when the musical magician twisted another half-circle and zapped her melody-making wand towards the audience. Slightly scared but full of belief, they bellowed out a boisterous chorus,

May you al–ways

love your

life!

The noise was rising line by line and so too was my pulse. Having missed the rehearsal, I had no idea when it was my turn. The first and third were always the same but each day, she changed the second and last line. Tabitha had already sung the second line, so I figured mine had to be next. Peering beneath the stage lights and out into the crowd, my heart fluttered as I noticed A.J.'s *belated* arrival.

"Just in time to cheer me on," I thought to myself before I spotted that she was not in a very "cheery" mood; her mouth was tight and sloping while her eyes looked rubbed and red. Although it was abundantly clear that she hadn't slept well, I didn't have time to rest either because the harpists began tickling their nylon strings the millisecond Mrs Mayhew threw her eyes upon them;

Pli! Li! Pli! Pli!

Li! Pli!

Pli!

A sound straight from the heavens descended upon the hall while I felt like I was falling into hell. Because my breathing was so heavy, there wasn't room in my mouth for words. As I looked up, the musical demon with the fiery baton was pointing right at me.

Silence.

Silence hung everywhere apart from in my chest as my heart pounded like it was about to blow a hole through my Dismal-Air blazer. Doing her best to encourage me, Mrs Mayhew smiled her warmest smile and nodded my way but, fear froze every inch of my body. Despite looking longingly towards A.J. for some sort of smile or nod of reassurance, her gaze was fixed to the floor while everyone stared straight at me. I flicked my tongue and unclenched my jaw in the hope that the line might magically fall out, but the stubborn silence refused to budge.

Lowering her baton, Mrs Mayhew had no option but to open her arms and invite the rest of the choir to sing my line,

And love ev-ery

thing you

do!

It might have been thirteen mouths and twenty-six lips, but it sounded like it was twice as many compared to the silence seeping from me. The urge to run was nudging me from the stage but I was determined to fight it. To not give up. I wanted to repay Mrs Mayhew and prove to everyone who doubted her just how amazing she was and show them how much she had helped me. My mouth was locked but my feet were anchored.

The cellists bounced into action without requiring Mrs Mayhew's signal. As they swung and rolled their delicate bows across those tubby strings, they generated deep, deep vibrations of sound,

Woov! Wuuv! Woov! Woov!

Wuv! Woov!

Woov!

The musical marvel then spun around so fast she almost forgot her feet which still pointed the other way. Flinging her hands through the air, she beckoned the frightened but fascinated audience to play their part. With ear-piercing passion, they accepted.

May you al - ways

live your

life!

Every word shot from their mouths as if they were spitting out big, buzzing wasps. Sharpening her baton against the air, the tiny head-teacher pointed towards the trumpeters who were poised to spit,

Parp! Purp! Purp! Parp!

Parp! Purp!

Parp!

Whisking frantically back to the choir like they were cupcakes left too long in the oven, Mrs Mayhew momentarily crouched down towards the floor before launching back up into the air. Manically, she shook her arms and waved her hands as if ten thousand volts just shot through her body. Tiny Timmy Weismark who was standing directly in front of me was now the target of her electric-eel baton. This mad music mixer called on him to summon the next line from the very bottom of his belly,

May you nev-er

find it

dull!

The eyes of every row lit up as the most angelic voice soared from his lips. Everyone longed to hear more, but there wasn't a second to spare. Mrs Mayhew flicked her wrist back in the direction of the bass players with such enthusiasm that the baton flew right out of her hand and lodged itself in the strings of a bass guitar. Instantly, Mr Paradisi dashed across the stage to recapture the run-away stick. The unscheduled interval gave me the opportunity I needed to keep my promise to Mrs Mayhew.

While I whispered to the choir around me, the boys on bass grew impatient and added a little more rhythm to the revelling.

Bump! Bomp! Bump! Bomp!

Bump! Bump!

Bomp!

Mr Paradisi was still scampering back towards Mrs Mayhew who wasn't in the mood to wait. With only her fingers at her disposal, she shot her arms toward the choir and this time I was ready.

Ready like a volcano.

Ready to erupt.

As they heeded my request to fall silent, I exploded into a wild, full-blown, feverishly loud

MAY YOU LIVE IT
TO THE
FULL!

A warm rush of blood shot through my cheeks, tingling my skin as A.J. finally looked up from the floor. The mile-wide smile stretched across her face made me feel so light-headed and giddy, even the pockets of my blazer overflowed with joy.

Applause would have to wait. With baton back in hand, Mrs Mayhew directed her energy towards the drummers (*and guest drummer, Mr Paradisi*) who slammed out a collective,

Bam! Bam! Bam! Bam!

Bam! Bam!

Bam!

Bam!

Bam!

Bam!

Bam!

Mr Paradisi had waited so long for his moment he was reluctant to let it go.

Bam! Bam! Bam!

Bam! Bam!

Bam!

He continued with a cheeky grin while Mrs Mayhew shook her head and laughed. Even though it was already well past 9.15, Mr Paradisi seemed determined to keep Thursday morning's assembly going. Banging and bashing, he prolonged the racket until one of the boys yanked the drumstick from his hand.

"Awwww!" the audience groaned in mock sympathy. But the rhythmic fluff bomb didn't need a stick to play bang-bang. Spinning around, the cheeky meerkat smashed the drum with his frisky, frolicking tail. A roar of uncontrollable laughter rose up from the crowd below who laughed so hard a few slipped from their seats.

Bam! Bam! Bam!

Bam! Bam!

Bam!

He continued to butt-drum until a sharp and stern finger click from Mrs Mayhew broke him from his bum-drumming day-dream.

"Awww!" the crowd consoled as poor Paradisi swung his head down around his shoulders in shame. With the small hand of the assembly hall clock signalling twenty past nine, morning lessons were overdue yet nobody wanted the madness to end. Not least the young girl sitting in the back row who suddenly stood up from her chair, cupped her hands around her mouth and shouted,

"We want more! We want more!"

It didn't take long for those around her to join in. With a blinding-bunch of Christmas morning smiles backing her into a corner, Mrs Mayhew had the excuse she needed to grant the wowed crowd the encore they 'demanded'.

Half-facing the musicians and half-facing the audience, she once again crashed her hands against the air. This time it wasn't choir, then musicians, then audience. This time it was anyone and everyone in unison.

Together.

May you al-ways

live your

life!

Bam!

Dung! Twang!

Duff!

Parp! Pli! Woov!

Apart from the sneering snides, too cool to join in, every other mouth and finger and heart and hand that was in any way connected to Thrive Academy was locked and lost in a pulsing whirl of song and music.

I sang louder than them all.

Ev-ery day try

some-thing

new!

Twang!

Parp! Woov!

Pli! Clong! Bang! Wump!

The same seven notes, the same four lines looped and whirled around our ears but every time they came, they were bigger and brighter and more powerful than before.

May you al-ways

love your

life!

Parp!

Pli! Bam!

Wamp! Woov! Twang! Twung!

This little song that had squeaked out of the lightly lip-sticked mouth of Mrs Mayhew on Monday morning was becoming something truly special. This simple, little ditty was growing day by day into something more than a song; it was becoming an anthem.

And love ev-ery

thing you

do!

Twung!

Bam! Pli!

Wamp! Woov! Clang! Parp!

The last line. The closing line. The line that brought this marvellously bonkers assembly to a halt was delivered with such ferocious gusto, it must have registered on the Richter scale. Each and every student who whacked and strummed and plucked and blew out musical notes did so with such devoted determination that the walls of the hall had to stretch upward and bend outward in order to keep all that insane energy inside.

At 9.25, Mrs Mayhew turned and led the bona fide members of the brand new *Thrive Academy Orchestra & Choir* to the front of the stage to take a bow. As I stood there, the applause was so intense and so deafening, it pulsed through me like a second heart.

A second heart with a second song.

16

Lips Unzipped

"**H**ow come you were late?" I inquired while trying to catch up with a speed-walking A.J.

Without turning towards me, she shrugged and marched on. If the turnstiles hadn't been removed, I'm sure she would have vaulted over them.

"Did your alarm not go off 'cause you forgot to charge up your banana phone?" I joked in the hope of resuscitating her smile.

Although her every glance and twitch begged me not to mention yesterday's events, I felt obliged to at least try to part the storm clouds brewing behind her eyes,

"Don't let them get you down," I consoled. It was a line I'd heard from so many, so often but it was a line I scarcely believed myself.

As A.J. nodded a brief, reluctant nod, I suddenly realised how utterly infuriating it was to converse with someone who doesn't talk back. For three years, I was the chief shrugger; I was the expert nodder; but now A.J. had transformed into SUPER-CAPTAIN SHRUG'N'NOD.

"Was my singing loud enough? I hoped that last line would blow your eyelashes clean off!" I continued to ramble, determined to clear the fog. Although the corner of her mouth briefly lifted half an inch, A.J. seemed more dispirited than an electronic toy with fast-fading batteries.

Thursday's timetable boasted a musical feast for every age and interest: in the morning we were treated to a *Paint Your Own Mini-Guitar Workshop* before Hector, a Spanish-guitar maker, walked us through the history of the six-string. With the help of a short video, he also explained the hours and skill it took to make just one plus-size ukulele.

Briskly, I coated my guitar with black and red butterflies while A.J. listlessly painted hers in green, yellow, red and black stripes. It was a striking but strange choice and when anybody asked what the colours meant she shrugged a listless "dunno." Despite Jarvis and his posse staying out of our way, A.J. regularly scanned the room to check they were a safe distance.

At break-time, we were greeted by the same giant chalkboard that met us after Tuesday morning's record-breaking assembly. Upon the black slate, flashes of white chalk announced,

What Instrument Would You Like to Play?

Choose your two-hour workshop!

Room 1 – Drums

Room 2 – Guitar

Room 3 – Piano

Room 4 – Violin

Room 5 – Saxophone

Room 6 – Bass Guitar

No experience necessary!

"We have to do saxophone!" I announced giddily while wondering if the bright, brass object I was picturing in my head was in fact a saxophone and not a trombone or a trumpet. Displaying little enthusiasm for any option, A.J. stood back from the crowd, and allowed everyone else to gather around the musical menu.

"Which workshop would you like?" I asked, desperate to ensure we signed up for the same one.

As her brown curls bobbed above yet another shrug, my frustration grew and my temper popped by to say "Hi!" A.J.'s gloom wasn't the only thing winding me up. It was everything: Blafferty! The Bonsons! Plus the stinkingly-rubbish possibility that tomorrow morning's assembly might be Mrs Mayhew's last. Just as I tried to send my temper back into hiding, Jarvis and his jolly jesters barged their way through the crowd.

As he and his flock scanned the chalk-board and raved about who wanted to do what, A.J. cowered behind me, longing to disappear.

"That's three votes for guitar and four for

drums, so drums it is!" Jarvis declared before they all turned to leave, "I doubt the vote's going to be that close tomorrow night!" he sniped as he passed me and my silent shadow.

The saxophone workshop was fun, and by the end, I could play "Three Blind Mice" (with one or two clumsy parps mixed in) while A.J. was too saddled with sadness to even try. Though she pushed the brass keys and made the odd attempt to blow into the mouth of the sax as the tutor drew near, her head and heart were someplace else.

"I want to go home," she unexpectedly whispered a few minutes before lunch.

"You don't feel well?" I asked, oblivious to what she meant, "You should ask Mrs Murphy if someone can pick you up."

"No. Not that home. My mum's home. Her birth-home. Where I can blend in and disappear and not always be seen as...as...different," she revealed without looking up from the floor.

"But I can't go with you. I'm a red-head. I'll burn!" I joked, not knowing what else to say.

Despite her best attempts to resist the urge, A.J. finally laughed. At first, it was a little baby- laugh but when she glanced up towards me and took a good look at my white, translucent skin, she laughed some more. In fact, we both laughed so hard; the tutor had to convey his displeasure with a Hollywood frown and an over-pronounced "SSSSHHH!"

"Well, that was different!" I whispered as Mr Shush dropped his scowl and turned away.

"What?" A.J. asked, still smiling.

"Me being told to be quiet!"

A loud, unstoppable chuckle lurched from the bottom of A.J.'s stomach while I hooted so hard, it became one of those strange, silent laughs that made no noise until the very end when it all falls out like an eruption of lunacy.

"You two! Go stand outside and calm yourselves down! I won't ask again!" the Shush-Shush Man insisted.

By the end of lunch, the clouds were clearing, her battery levels were rising, and A.J. was returning to normal. Well, her 'normal' anyway. The fact that all the playground chatter revolved around yesterday's Evening News and Friday night's vote provided the perfect distraction.

"Are students allowed to go to the meeting?" A.J. asked while unpeeling the latest model of the banana phone.

"No, dad said it's just for governors," Sebastian clarified before warning, "which means the golden tie gang will probably get their way."

"Why?" A.J. inquired.

"Nearly all of their mums and dads are parent governors and we know how they'll be voting," Sebastian clarified.

"Well, then it's back to text-book Blafferty," A.J. summarised with a sigh.

As Seb and A.J. spoke, an idea struck me. An idea that was so good, even Google couldn't think of it,

"You should ask him if a few of us could say a few words to represent the student view or at least write something that could be read out," I suggested.

"Yeah, let's do that!" A.J. squealed as the oomph and energy she usually bristled with finally returned.

"It's worth a try. I'll ask him tonight," Seb avowed.

For the last session of the day, Mrs Murphy directed Year 6 towards her classroom where she introduced us to a smiling, bearded man who stood before a long line of brown, black and navy cases of various shapes and sizes.

"Afternoon everyone. Today Mrs Mayhew has arranged a visit from someone who is famous for one very special reason. Gustav is a musical genius from Romania who has, over the last twenty years, travelled the globe searching for strange, new instruments. After thousands of miles of travelling and searching and learning, he can now play over three hundred different instruments. Isn't that amazing?" she asked while we all nodded with wide eyes. "So, without further ado, I give you Gustav."

"Thank you, Miss Murpy, for your kindness introduction," the tall man replied in a thick Eastern European accent. Because his words didn't quite communicate what he was trying to say, the petty Giggle Gang couldn't help but titter every time he faintly confused a word.

"Great afternoon everyone!" he smiled with a wave of his hand and a slight bow of his head.

"Good afternoon Gustav!" half of us replied noisily enough to mask the chuckling of our ill-mannered 'friends'. If I was Mrs Murphy, I would have immediately invited Jarvis up to the front and made him apologise to Gustav in Romanian. After he failed to do that, I would then lock him in a ten-hour detention until he learned how to say, "I sincerely apologise Gustav" in perfect Romanian so he could appreciate how difficult it was to learn a foreign language and not judge other so quickly. However, as Gustav continued to speak, Jarvis continued to snicker, and Mrs Murphy continued to do nothing,

"Now, the first instrument I ever learned to playing was the tin whistle ... when I was three. When I was five ... I learned to playing the piano ... but it was not until my first holiday to Turkey when I was seven that I starting my collection," he announced before reaching down to retrieve a flat rectangular case from the floor.

For the most part, it looked like an ordinary briefcase except for one sliced off corner which made it seem like a half-eaten, leather-bound sandwich. (Yum □)

"This is the qanun!" he announced before unclipping the case and removing a bizarre string instrument that looked like a guitar and a piano had been fused together by a mad musical scientist.

After sliding his index fingers into two long, metal plectrums, Gustav played a strange, hypnotic sound. Well, it was strange until the fifth note when we realised why it sounded so familiar; it was Mrs Mayhew's assembly song.

"Ah... you knowing that one ... eh? Mrs Mayhew teaching me it this morning!" he laughed while continuing to pluck the tiny strings.

We all sat and stared as Gustav showcased his armoury of instruments. There was the Sarod from Afghanistan, the Ban Suri from Sri Lanka, the Thumb Piano from Zimbabwe and many, many more exotic objects that produced weird and wonderful sounds (all to the same seven-beat tune!). After Gustav introduced each member of his musical family, he invited us to choose one and practise playing on it while he walked around, helping us to understand how to make it purr.

After a shaky start, it looked like the day was going to end on a high. A.J. smiled and giggled as she played on her thumb piano while I failed miserably to master the Irish Bouzouki.

"I wonder if I could sneak this home without ol' Gus noticing," A.J. dared as she plucked the edges of the tinchy, metal chords.

"Yours makes the most beautiful sound," I replied while creating the opposite with my big onion-shaped guitar.

"It's like a piano made for baby angels," she swooned.

With ten minutes remaining, Mrs Murphy was summoned to the main office for an urgent phone call. With Gustav left to fend for himself, thirty feverishly excited ten and eleven-year-olds continued to play with their tuneful (and tuneless) toys.

"Can I asking you all to sitting down in a semi-circle with your instruments?" he asked with a toothy smile.

Once we were in position, he provided the next instruction, "So, now you knowing me, but I would like to knowing you. One by one, can you please telling me your name and why you choosing your instrument?"

A.J. and I were the last two on the far end of the semi-circle while Jarvis and Simon sat directly opposite us at the start of the half-moon.

"So, let's starting with you young man!" Gustav directed with a flick of his wrist towards Jarvis.

"My name is .... A.J.," the blonde-topped bully suddenly announced to a muddle of giggles and gasps, "I having no friends, and I choosing this instrument because it looking the easiest to playing," he revealed with a snide smile while I leaned my shoulder into A.J.'s, silently supporting her.

"Okay, thanking you A.J. ... and I hoping you making some friends soon," Gustav naively replied, having no idea what was really happening.

"Next you?" he proceeded by pointing at Simon.

Simon didn't reply because he was too busy fetching something from his bag. After retrieving a piece of crumpled paper, he quickly scribbled something in thick, black marker which caused Jarvis', due to his sneak-preview viewing angle, to reel backwards in a cupped-hand titter. Holding the paper aloft, Simon swivelled left and right to ensure everyone, sitting and standing, could see. It read,

"My name's Willow and I'm too lazy to talk."

Instantly, I jolted forward but A.J. barred me with her arm and growled through clenched teeth, "Don't give them the satisfaction."

"Somebody has to say something," I whispered through an exasperated frown but A.J. turned away from my gaze and shook her head NO!

Finally, a red-faced Gustav sensed his game had been hijacked, "Okay then Willow, I won't asking you to saying anymore. Why don't we telling everyone why we choosing our instruments instead of saying our names," Gustav instructed. Without warning, A.J. shouted a sharp and assured,

"NO!"

A sea of stunned faces spun in her direction. Staring straight through Jarvis, she rose from the floor and declared in a booming, unruffled tone,

"My name is ..."

Suddenly she stopped. Her breathing was heavy and her eyes darted from face to face until she bit her lip, clenched her fists and began again,

"My names is ... Anodiwa Jabulani Jones and I chose this instrument because my mother is from Zimbabwe and so too is the better half of me. Every time I play it, I imagine my grandparents and ancestors making these beautiful sounds which transport me to my mother's birthplace: a place she loves: a place I love - a place I am proud to call home."

A.J. (or Anodiwa as she was now known) stared Jarvis down, forcing his face to fill with a blood-red-flush. Her clenched fists and firmly set jaw distinctly communicated, "Come on! What else have you got? Bring on your next cheap trick and nasty comment!"

Though it was quite clear, he wouldn't, Mrs Murphy's return meant the coward didn't have the option.

"I'm so sorry about that Gustav. There was an urgent call. I do hope everyone has behaved themselves," she asked with an air of suspicion.

"Yes! Yes!" Gustav replied with a slight hesitation.

"Willow, can I have a word outside for a second, please? The rest of you start packing up before we say goodbye to Gustav," she instructed, prompting everyone to stand up and return their instruments to their strange-shaped cases.

My heart hammered against my chest while I waited for Mrs Murphy to join me outside. Her mouth was dry as she spoke, "Willow, I've just had a call ... and eh ... there's been an accident ... and your dad ... well, he can't pick you up."

17

One Night at Anodiwa's

There were no words.

I should have screamed or sobbed or both, but I didn't. Instead, I slumped to the floor as if someone had suddenly unplugged me.

"What's the matter, Willow?" Mrs Murphy asked with a wrinkled brow until it suddenly hit her, "Oh no! Your dad's fine. He's absolutely fine," she quickly clarified (though not quickly enough). "I've just spoken to him. There's been a pile-up on the A-twelve so he's gone with his truck to try and clear it but he fears he might be there for some time."

Though I'm obviously no expert in the art of language, I did think Mrs Murphy could have chosen her words more carefully. As the tidal wave of grief swelling through my body slowly drifted back out to shore, I tried to tune in to the exact purpose of her patter.

"So, he's asked me to tell you that he's arranged for you to go home with A.J. Her mum is expecting you."

For a second, I genuinely believed I had lost my father, but in reality, I had gained an evening at my best friend's house: and what an evening it was.

After inhaling a delicious bowl of dovi which was *the* best (and only) peanut-butter stew I had ever tasted, A.J. and I pounded the twelve carpeted stairs to her room.

"You've been painting butterflies?" I burst as she welcomed me through her bedroom door with a wave of her arm.

"Yeah, five different types since yesterday but so far, I can't seem to magic them into life," she joked before clicking her fingers at the pink winged wonder resting upon the easel that blocked the window, "see? Nothing!"

"So what do I call you now?" I asked with

a slight hesitation after flouncing into a purple bean bag by the end of her bed.

"Anodiwa at school but A.J. when it's just you and me," she replied in an assured tone, "I picked A.J. because I thought Anodiwa Jabulani was too long and too awkward for everyone to say but I don't care anymore. Now I want everyone to know how proud I am of my name."

"What does it mean?" I inquired, genuinely intrigued.

"Ha!" she replied with a slight blush. "Anodiwa means the loved one and Jabulani means rejoice!"

"That's so much better than my name – I'm a tree that gets turned into cricket bats," I joked as we both giggled, "so … how are we going to save Mrs Mayhew?"

"We could change the locks on the school gate," she suggested with a wry smile, "if Blafferty can't get in the building, he can't ruin our day."

"I wish it was that easy," I admitted as I flossed the brown, threaded hair of a well-worn rag doll through my fingers.

"We need a plan!" A.J. determined before springing from her bed and flipping open a fresh sheet of paper on her easel.

"We need a five-step plan to save Mrs Mayhew!" I chimed while struggling to depart the bean bag in the same spritely fashion that she had left her bed. (Don't judge me – bean bags are soft-cushioned death holes)

"Number one!" A.J. shouted after popping the lid off a light blue felt-tip, "We let the world see how amazing Mrs Mayhew is which we will achieve by ... by ..."

"Seb's dad convincing the chair of governors to let us speak," I suggested to help finish her sentence.

"Yes, but we'll need more than that. We need to..." A.J. repeated, yet again creating a drawn-out hush while we awaited the blinding idea that we hoped was *belated* in its arrival,

"...we kidnap Mr Blafferty and send him on a one-way flight to China!" she screamed before turning to scribble her 'brilliant' idea upon the blank page.

"Eh, he is a very tall man and last time I checked, flights to China were quite expensive," I sternly replied.

"Oh yeah. You're right," A.J. reasoned, scratching out her first idea, "then why don't we kidnap all the golden-tie parents and send them on a one-way ticket to the Isle of Man!"

Again, A.J. was scrawling word for word what she had just said until I walked up behind her and pinched the marker from her wriggling fist.

"Can we try something that doesn't involve kidnapping?" I proposed while she slapped at my hand, desperate to retrieve the marker.

"We can build our own school and appoint Mrs Mayhew as our head-teacher!" A.J. squealed before abandoning the blue and fetching a dark, yellow from her desk.

"Where exactly will we get the million pounds to buy bricks and desks and ceilings from?" I inquired while attempting to yank the latest marker from her grasp.

"My brother! He has hundreds of bricks!" she yelled in a frantic, breathy tone.

"Really? Isn't he like three years old?" I questioned.

"Yeah, he is, but he genuinely has thousands and thousands of bricks," she insisted while committing the first step of our "plan" to paper.

"By any chance, are these Lego bricks?" I probed like a very clever detective.

"Yeah, they're so easy to click together," she replied without the slightest hint of sarcasm.

As I finally wrenched marker #2 from her hand, I made a bold suggestion, "Why don't we sit and talk and then when we come up with an idea that doesn't involve kidnapping grown men or whole groups of people or making a school out of Lego, maybe then we write our idea on the pad. Sound good?"

As A.J. turned from the easel towards me, it was impossible not to notice her tear glossed eyes.

"We can't let her leave," she sobbed before snapping the rag-doll from my left hand and hugging it to her chest, "if he comes back, he will ruin everything and not only for us who are leaving soon but for the little ones like my brother who starts next year and for anyone who's just as weird as you and me. We have to do it for all of them! Everyone must know how amazing Mrs Mayhew is!" she professed, blinking her damp eyes dry.

"That's our first step," I smiled while moving towards the easel with the confiscated marker, "Number 1! We show the world just how amazing Mrs Mayhew is."

"But how?" A.J. asked while flouncing onto her bed before instantly rebounding back up and squealing, "I've got it!"

"NO KIDNAPPING!" I warned.

"No! No! No kidnapping! Well, we could kidnap her, but I don't think we'll need to. We should invite that reporter from the local news to see tomorrow's morning assembly and that way everyone will see how amazing Mrs Mayhew is. She's been following the story all week; she'll definitely be interested."

"But how do we invite her?" I asked.

"Email!" A.J. spat back like it was the most blindingly obvious idea.

"We can't. Students can't just invite anyone to walk into the school. It would have to be from the principal or another teacher," I warned.

"That's it!" A.J. burst like an exploding star.

Without saying a word, she reached under her pillow and pulled out her phone (an actual smartphone – not a banana). Her face was lit with a dim yellow light as she rolled her thumb across the screen. This bath-bomb of fizzing energy so enthralled me; I didn't even bother to ask what she was up to. Before I could, she was pressing a long sequence of numbers into the touch screen,

"Hello and good evening," she suddenly drawled in a voice that wasn't her own, "this is Mrs Mayhew, the head-teacher of Thrive Academy."

I am not particularly sure what keeps eyeballs from falling out but whatever magical science is at work, the actions of this daring impersonator put my eye-sockets to the test.

"I was wondering if I could speak to Emily Nouveaux?" the mimic asked while blinking a wink my way.

A whizzing shiver ran down my spine as I ran towards A.J., flounced down by her bedside and rested my arms upon her deceitful knees. Silence settled for a second before I widened my eyes, opened my palms and squared my shoulders which was the internationally recognised code for "what on earth is going on?"

"Oh, that's a shame," A.J. finally blurted, briefly forgetting the posh and poised voice with which she started the conversation, "well if it would please you, could you kindly leave her a communication?"

Mrs Mayhew was only in her thirties but A.J. was acting like she was born in 1933.

"Could you kindly inform her that she is cordially invited to my assembly tomorrow morning at Thrive Academy? She will not be required to ring through from the gate; she can enter with the children at eight fifty-five. I will be pleased to converse with her at the conclusion of the assembly ... oh, that's wonderful ... thank you so much for your time, I'm ever so grateful."

Dropping her phone, A.J. fell back on the bed and squealed with laughter. Pulling at the sleeve of her jumper, I begged, "Tell me! Tell me! What did they say? Is she coming?"

A.J. laughed so loud and so long, I could hardly make out what she was saying. Eventually, I learned that Emily was currently investigating something else but the receptionist would pass on the message, and she's sure Emily would be very interested in visiting the school tomorrow morning.

"We've done it!" A.J. squealed. "Blafferty will never be allowed back into that building once everyone sees Mrs Mayhew's assembly with their own eyes - even if it's through their TV."

While we didn't quite manage the five step plan we set out to achieve, we did have one - one step that gave us a fighting chance of saving Mrs Mayhew.

Just after nine, dad rang to say he was on his way back but he would be at least another hour. Mr. and Mrs. Jones told him to take his time and kindly offered to put me up for the night and get me to school in the morning.

Despite being considerably taller than A.J., her pyjamas still fit me reasonably well. That night, as I lay in the silent darkness beneath unfamiliar sheets, the "top" to A.J.'s toe, I yearned for mum to return and sing me to sleep but 12.5 seconds later, I was wishing something else entirely.

I wished I hadn't lent my headphones to Seb because A.J. snored like a pig sawing planks.

18

Grand Finale?

When I awoke the next morning, it took me two yawns and three stretches to remember where I was. Wafts of grilled meat and toasted bread seeped through the gap in the door as I ruffled the warm quilt, hoping to stir the still-snoozing, still-snoring A.J. The moment she stirred, she shot upright in the bed like a re-animated corpse,

"LET'S GET KIDNAPPING!" she bellowed despite her eyes being half-sealed with sleep.

Leaping out from beneath her duvet, she grabbed a dressing gown and flung it my way.

"Come on side-kick! Later, we will save the day but before that - BREAKFAST!" she grinned while funnelling her arms through the soft, pink sleeves of her 'favourite' gown.

"Is that your super-hero costume?" I asked while swivelling my legs out from beneath the warm sheets.

"State of the art, indestructible polyester! Bomb-proof! Bullet-proof and Blafferty-proof!" she joked before galloping out the door.

A five-star 'hotel' breakfast (which put my usual bowl of dry, bland cereal to shame) was waiting upon the kitchen table when we arrived downstairs. While I 'politely' devoured mine, A.J.'s mouth was full of other things,

"We can't let him win! Whatever Mrs Mayhew does on that stage today, we must show her our support and let her know that moaning whinger isn't ever coming back! She is our head-teacher, and she is never leaving!" A.J. rambled while holding her sausage-topped fork in a slightly threatening manner.

After scooping up scrambled egg with mine, I opened my mouth to reply, but A.J.'s mum beat me to it. As she tumbled a fresh tower of warm, buttery toast upon the table, she advised, "Make sure you two enjoy the day you do have with Mrs Mayhew. Do not waste it worrying about all the days you could have had. Today is the greatest day because it's here. You have to remember yesterday and wait for tomorrow but today only asks you to live and love the right now."

"We will mum," A.J. replied with a tender smile which stirred an unexpected flush of envy to prickle through me. Jealousy was something I rarely felt, but in that moment, I would have given anything to sit at my kitchen table to have one more round of tea and toast with my mum.

By 8.25, we were dressed in our Dismal-Air uniforms and strolling towards the school gate. The curtain was about to drop on a marvellous week of mind-boggling assemblies, and I prayed that our special guest would accept the 'invitation' to the finale,

"She better be here!" A.J. moaned before waving towards Sebastian who stood uneasily on the edges of the rambling crowd, "And don't tell anyone what we've done. Not even Seb. You know what he's like with rules and things, he won't understand," she warned as I mimed zipping my lips shut and throwing away the key.

The instant Seb spotted us, he immediately sprinted our way, "A.J.! Willow! Dad said yes!" he panted.

"Yes? About what?" I asked, confused and groggy from a broken night's sleep.

"Yes about the meeting. Mrs Deehan said we can speak tonight. Right at the very start, we'll have two minutes each to tell the governors what we think," he explained while A.J. squealed and fist bumped the air.

"That's amazing, but I'll have to ask dad if I can go," I said, slightly dampening the excitement.

"Don't worry! My dad said he would talk to him today," Seb added as he fetched my headphones from his bag and held them towards me, "here, these are yours."

"Step two is complete!" A.J. wheezed

while skipping towards the school gate.

"Step two?" Sebastian asked, "what was step one?"

"Oh, don't worry," I said, scrambling for the first lie that popped into my head, "you know what A.J.'s like at maths."

By 8.45, there was still no sign of Ms Nouveaux, and Bradley could not shut up about the teacher who didn't talk,

"Anyone wanna bet?" he asked while rotating around the crowd, "anyone wanna bet me that our supply head-teacher is actually going to talk?"

Most students tutted and told him to "get lost" however, one unexpected voice accepted the challenge,

"I bet you one hundred pounds that Mayhew *does* speak today!" Jarvis Bonson declared before holding out a firm right hand to strike the deal.

"Eh," a wobbly handed Bradley stuttered, finally lost for words and struggling to think of where he could nab £100 from. But as they say, a fool and his money (that he doesn't even have) are easily parted, "eh, okay. You're on!" he feebly grinned while reaching out his trembling hand to seal the deal.

"I bet you one hundred pounds that Mrs Mayhew **will** speak today. She has to! It would be rude of her to leave without saying goodbye!" Jarvis smiled while his slithering shadows snickered.

As the school gates opened and the crowd ambled through, A.J. and I lingered back in the hope of spotting our guest, but there was no sign of the reporter and her cameraman.

"Looks like it's over before it's even begun," A.J. sighed as we reluctantly walked towards the assembly hall.

"Let's wait another minute – it's only five to nine," I consoled, pretending to be strong.

"But she's not expecting to meet us, is she? She's expecting to meet Mrs Mayhew," A.J. barked with a hint of irritation in her voice.

"You're right. Sorr ...sorry," I chirped with a slight stutter. For so long, I couldn't find any words, but it was still going to be some time before I found the right word in situations like that. Regardless, I tried again, "like your mum said this morning, let's make sure we enjoy today's assembly," I optimistically proposed though A.J. wasn't listening as she stomped off towards the hall.

When I finally caught up with her, I was surprised to find her chatting to Mr Paradisi. The fur-ball assistant was standing inside the entrance, struggling to grasp a tiny, wooden clipboard within his furry hands.

"Looks like we're in for a good one!" A.J. smiled as she struck the clipboard with a rope-tied pencil that swung away from her and towards me, "Emily has to see this."

Intrigued, I edged towards Mr Paradisi. Upon the clipboard a long list of names was scrawled with empty columns running alongside. Option A read, "SOMETHING SAVOURY" while

Option B offered "SOMETHING SWEET".

Having devoured eggs, bacon and enough toast to feed a rhino, I should have been full, but I still fancied a little nibble of "something sweet".

After I ticked Option B, Mr Paradisi retrieved the clipboard and scuttled off towards the stage. A sweet mix of soothing aromas filled my nostrils the instant I entered the assembly hall. It usually smelt of musty curtains, cleaning products and body odour (especially when it was hot 🔥😖) but this was something very different. Everyone was speculating what these "sweet" and "savoury" treats might be.

"I hope it's warm waffles with chocolate chip ice cream!" A.J. swooned while Bradley tried his best to ruin the mood.

"She's trying to buy us off. She really has no shame," he whinged.

Thankfully the strange sounds from behind the curtain were drowning out Mr I LOVE CONSPIRACIES. Sizzling, popping and rattling noises seeped out from beneath the heavy, blue velvet and crept into our ears, whetting our appetites even more.

At the stroke of nine, the long curtains whipped back and there she was; Mrs Mayhew, standing in front of a half-moon kitchen cluttered with hot plates, toasters, ovens and heaps and heaps of yummy things. Her digestive-coloured hair bounced a little as she lightly treaded her way to the front of the assembly hall stage. As it was Friday, her pleated skirt and spectacles were painted flamingo pink while shiny raspberry ribbons laced her smart, black shoes, and a ring of rosy pearls encircled her neck.

Although Monday's sensational tap-dancing felt like months ago, the manic mixture of sadness and giddiness flopping and flipping around my stomach told me I wasn't ready to say goodbye.

Upon raising her right hand, Mr Paradisi scuttled towards her, carrying a mini-whiteboard. Written upon this small, shining rectangle in thick, black marker was a most wonderful question which caused 188 hungry hands to rocket into the air,

Who's hungry?

"See? Her monkey has to talk for her," Bradley lashed before being promptly shushed.

"Look!" A.J. said, frantically prodding my shoulder.

A quick snap of my neck to the right allowed me to see why she was breathing a deep sigh of relief.

"She's here!" A.J. beamed while the corners of my eyes moistened with an unexpected tear.

Our plan was working; Emily Nouveux and her cameraman were poised along the wall just a few rows behind us, ready to report and record. But Mrs Mayhew had spotted the "invited" intruders, and her wrinkled brow suggested she was not pleased. Mrs Murphy was also on high alert and travelling their way.

"Excuse me, what are you doing here?"

she asked in a heavy whisper.

Though most people were still facing forward awaiting Mrs Mayhew's next move, everyone around me had tuned their radio into Mrs Murphy's conversation with the *mysterious* visitors.

Grabbing my hand, A.J. crossed my fingers before re-crossing her own. Sucking down big gulps of air, she looked like she was about to jump from a sky-high plane, "Please! Please! Please!" she murmured.

"Mrs Mayhew called the office last night to invite us to her assembly," Emily informed a surprised Mrs Murphy.

"You spoke to her yourself?" the teacher asked with a rising level of disbelief.

"Well not exactly, she left a message with the receptionist," the journalist clarified.

"Ah, that explains it," the teacher replied without explaining what had been explained.

Turning back towards the stage, Mrs Murphy flicked a double thumbs up which seemed to soften the wrinkles in Mrs Mayhew's frown and allowed A.J. and I to breathe out two large sighs of relief.

Step 1 had begun.

All we could do now was pray for her final assembly to be as SUPER-BONKERS-INSANE as possible to make sure it made the top story on the evening news and wow the world (or at least our governors.) Of course, before anything else could begin, Mrs Mayhew had a song to sing: a hotly-anticipated song. Many of those sitting around me were already tapping the beat on their legs with their fidgety fingers.

As she began to sing, the tiny teacher was only audible for the first letter of the first word of the opening line (the M) before the rowdy chorus joined in and drowned her out. We were louder than ever,

"May you always live your life,"

"Don't give up, don't give in," as this was new, we fell silent.

"May you always love your life," again

we were back, loud and lively.

"Stay the course, and you will win", this was also new so many of us mumbled along trying to guess what might rhyme with "in". I correctly plumped for "win" while Sebastian aimed and missed with "begin".

After the song was sung, the tiny head-teacher strolled inside her half-moon kitchen, popped a pink apron over her head and clapped her hands with a brisk double tap.

Right on cue, Mr Paradisi skipped out from the left of the stage sporting an "aww"-inducing white shirt and black bow tie. Just as we finished "aww"-ing, we were stunned to see another Mr Paradisi skip out from the right of the stage...

...then the left.

...then the right.

...again the left.

...again the right.

Our heads swivelled back and forth like we were watching a never-ending tennis-rally at Wimbledon.

"Please tell me you are seeing six Mr Paradisis?" Seb inquired while rubbing his clenched fists into his dazed eyes.

"They all look the same except for the different coloured bow ties." A.J. offered in equal bewilderment.

"Which one is Mr Paradisi then?" Seb wondered.

"What makes you think they're all Misters?" A.J. bit back.

Before any of us could answer, the black bow-tied Paradisi jumped upon the makeshift kitchen counter and held the clipboard aloft for the head-chef to see the first order of the morning. The other five dapper meerkats patiently awaited their cue.

Mrs Mayhew cleared her throat.

"She's going to speak," A.J. whispered while my heart throbbed with anticipation.

She lifted her top lip.

She lowered her bottom lip.

She breathed deep. But nothing came.

Nothing other than a gusty, shuddering exhale. 378 expectant eyes and one local news camera stared, unblinking. She cleared her throat again.

Top lip.

Bottom lip.

Breathe ... still nothing.

Looking to the floor, I clenched my teeth and re-crossed my fingers.

"Red light! Red light!" Sebastian whispered loud enough for the entire hall and half the schools in the country to hear.

Without warning, Mr Paradisi dropped his mini clipboard upon the counter and scampered up the arm of the tongue-tied little lady. Resting upon her right shoulder like a pirate's parrot, he tapped the side of Captain Mayhew's neck with his furry fingers.

Instantly, the head-teacher spoke,

"Order number one - something savoury,

Jar-vis, you may snick-er and tease,

but you will fly those planes with ease."

With that, she grabbed a knife and scythed a soft, white bap in half. Seizing a silver tongs, she snapped them closed and placed two slices of sizzling, crispy bacon upon the bed of soft, white bread as if she was laying them down for a nap. Without delay, she tapped her open hand on a tiny bell by the toaster and called, "Service!"

Green-tie Paradisi then leapt upon the countertop, grabbed a napkin and expertly wrapped it around the beautiful bacon bap before scampering towards Jarvis. He was closely followed by Red-tie Paradisi who carried a squeezy bottle of ketchup in one hand and a bottle of brown sauce in the other.

Giggles jiggled and ravenous eyes stared as Jarvis was fed first. A face-filling grin proved his delight and grew even greater once he realised that he now had a side order of one hundred pounds to go with his "something savoury". Smiling towards Bradley, he rubbed his thumb and forefingers together in a "show me the money" sign while chomping down on his freshly cooked breakfast.

"Order number two - something sweet,

Es-me Strutt has so much pa-ssion

... she will be the queen of fa-shion."

Esme smiled knowingly while Mrs Mayhew swivelled to her left, grabbed a spatula and flicked three small, brown discs into the air, one after another. A giddy wheeze rang around the hall as everyone realised what "something sweet" meant. In three quick moves, she scooped a stack of warm, fluffy pancakes onto a plate before Blue-tie Paradisi drizzled a bottle of liquid gold all over the plate. As soon as the maple syrup glistened beneath the bright, stage lights, the yellow-tied fluff-ball flung a handful of plump blueberries upon the tongue-tingling stack.

BING! went the bell as the head-teacher called "service" and Pink-tie Paradisi waddled off the stage with the pan-fried creation.

A.J. squeezed my hand and looked over

my shoulder, "They're going to love this. She's going to make breakfast for all of us, served by a team of specially trained meerkats."

"And magic!" I thought to myself while repeatedly blinking just to confirm that this bonkers banquet was actually happening.

"Do you think she's written and remembered a poem about all of us?" A.J. asked though all I could do was shrug as I watched Mrs Mayhew swiftly proceed along the front row, serving up breakfast and dishing out rhymes like the world's greatest (and first ever) chef-poet. Despite losing his bet, everyone could see that Bradley was, in some strange way, right about Mrs Mayhew (not that anyone would ever tell him). Just as I had noticed that day in her office, it was clear that talking didn't come easy. If it weren't for the Mr Paradisi's tapping and the rhyme at the end of each line, every word would likely be a tug-of-war between tongue and mind.

"Order thirty eight - something sweet,
though Figg-y is quite brash and so loud

on that west end stage, she'll wow the crowd."

The poetic principal was popping rhymes, filling baps and stacking pancakes at such a neck-cracking speed, her staff of meerkats were struggling to keep up. Blue Paradisi had mistakenly squirted ketchup all over a fresh batch of pancakes much to the delight of the audience. A slightly annoyed Mrs Mayhew shook her head and tutted before the glassy, apologetic eyes of the hairy blunderer melted her irritation.

BING!

"Service!" she hollered, summoning her fluffy soldier. They delivered the latest dish so speedily; they brought new meaning to the phrase "fast food".

"Order seventy four - something savoury,
Timmy, you are the most ten-a-cious of us all
you'll soon be sell-ing out the Roy-al Al-bert Hall."

As Timmy gratefully received his warm bacon bap, he beamed with a searchlight smile and shouted aloud, "Cheers Miss!" towards the twisting and spinning head-chef. Bradley turned around to share his latest theories with A.J., Seb and myself.

"That monkey is whispering to her, or I bet … I bet she's got a tiny ear-piece, and somebody is on the other end reading it to her. There's no way she knows all our names and all this stuff about us after only four days," he rambled, not realising his rhyme was next in line.

"Order one-two-seven - something sweet,"

But as Mrs Mayhew moved to speak, she stumbled, "B … B … B…" she stuttered while her sweat-glistened brow wrinkled and reddened beneath the eye of the watching TV camera. Something was sticking, her tongue was clicking. Despite Mr Paradisi's drumming, she could not reach the end of the word. With his mouth half-full of food, Timmy jumped to his feet and yelled,

"Don't worry Miss, there's no rush!"

As it was already ten past nine, there was indeed a rush, but inspired by Timmy's encouragement; a low chant began to grow within the centre of the crowd.

"What are they saying?" Bradley asked before the flicker suddenly caught fire and each word flamed brightly within our ears.

"May-hew!"

"May-hew!"

Feet stomped. Hands clapped,

"May-hew!"

"May-hew!

Hands clapped. Feet stomped.

"May-hew!"

"May-hew!

Not everyone was backing the boss, but as a warm smile grew across the head-teacher's face, the support was clearly working. Following the beat from the crowd, she tapped her tongs upon the counter, poured a fresh dollop of pancake mix upon the pan and tried again,

"Brad- ley ... you have - an inq-uis-it-ive mind,

Per-fect for sol-ving mill-ions of crimes."

Though I was sure Bradley would be uber-awkward and flat refuse to accept her poetic prediction about his possible career, he nodded rather vigorously in agreement. After accepting the stack of pancakes speared by a white, plastic fork, he stood up and announced,

"She's right! I don't know how but she's dead right. I'm gonna be a copper like my grandad."

Mrs Mayhew had re-discovered her rhythm and the minuscule rapper was heading our way,

BING!

"Service! Order one-two-three - something savoury,
Seb you are as smart as a co-llege pro-fess-or...
And will be the most won-der-ful risk ass-ess-or."

"I'm not sure what that is" Seb chirped, "but I quite like the sound of it!"

Before we could blink or think, the bell went *BING!* and A.J.'s number was up,

"Service! Order one-two-four - something sweet,
A.J. your hum-our al-ways does the trick
ea-sing the woes of the lon-ely and sick."

An easy chuckle rattled from my throat as I leaned into A.J. and hugged her. Without her humour, I would never have survived the long, dark days of Blafferty. As Mrs Mayhew held another syrup-drizzled stack of pancakes aloft, I knew I was up next. The *BING!* of the bell made my heart hop as she called,

"Service! Order one two five - something sweet,
Will-ow, this world's full of non-sense and noise,
Fill eve-ry ear with your beau-ti-ful voice."

Everyone nearby was munching and chewing and gobbling down their breakfast treats, but it wasn't my mouth that was full. It was my ears. They were filled with a most glorious sound; a sound I feared I might never hear again.

Mum was back.

Louder than ever.

Despite the racket of clashing frying pans and toasters and the sounds of teeth chomping and gnashing, I heard every word. *Her* every word - so loud and so clear.

"When you look up at the sky
Know that I'm not far."

So many emotions swirled through me that I feared I might explode. Jumping from my seat, I tipped my pancakes onto the floor, and ran from the row, right past Emily and her cameraman and through the doors of the assembly hall.

"She's back!" I screamed into the empty playground.

"She's back!" I screamed at nothing and no-one.

As I spun around, a large, black microphone and a peering camera lens greeted me,

"Who's back?" the reporter asked.

19

Flying Frog

Before Wednesday, I hadn't spoken for three years, and since Wednesday, I averaged less than thirty words a day, but with that microphone in front of me, I rambled like I was reporting the end of the world.

"I didn't speak for years because I was afraid of losing mum's lullaby...until Mrs Mayhew's painting came alive and all the butterflies fluttered above us...after I lost mum's lullaby, Mrs Mayhew told me a story about a melting snowball and promised me it would come back, and I believed her and she was right, it's just returned."

The poor journalist couldn't keep up. Her every question was met with a long-winded answer that gave rise to a million more questions.

Question? Blah!

Question? Blah! Blah!

Question? Blah! Blah! BLAH!

For ten whole minutes, my mouth drooled and dribbled words like a busted tap. The tsunami of syllables only stopped when my well-fed friends poured out of the hall and into the playground. The second she was free of the door, A.J. dashed towards us,

"Will we make it on this evening's news?" she asked Emily with a 'pretty please' eyelash flutter.

"Hopefully. I'll show it to my editor once I get back and it will be up to them but there's been a lot of interest in this story so it should make air," Emily replied as we walked her towards reception.

Moments after waving them goodbye, the Bradley shaped shadow that had been lingering nearby assaulted us with another round of mouth bullets, "I can see what your plan is but even if it does make the evening news, it's going to be the last story before the weather meaning it won't be on TV until six fifty five at the earliest. If the meeting in the village hall starts at seven, nobody's going to see it."

The usual "ha-ha" which accompanied everything Bradley ever said was absent. He seemed genuinely concerned about the governors missing the assembly footage.

"Unless they make it the top story at six thirty - that might be early enough for them to see it," he added before slumping off across the playground.

A.J. and I looked on in disbelief, "I think the free breakfast has finally won him over," she suggested.

"Or maybe he's grieving for the one hundred pounds he's just lost," I ventured as A.J. laughed.

Throughout the rest of the day, we rotated around different rooms in our year groups. Until little break, we baked decorative cupcakes in the school canteen with Miss Patton who modelled how to pipe pink-icing into a swirling, ascending staircase.

"Mine doesn't look like a staircase. It looks more like something my dog does in the back garden," A.J. joked before scrapping her first attempt and starting again.

Once we mastered our swirling staircases, Miss demonstrated how to create perfectly dipped, chocolate strawberries which were to sit upon the pink icing. Despite wrinkle browed warnings about not sampling the hot chocolate sauce ourselves, we couldn't resist.

"Who's going to want to eat a strawberry that someone's used as a chocolate sauce sponge?" Miss Patton teased before finally caving in and joining us, "But then, who cares? This chocolate sauce is too good!"

After break, Mrs Murphy wobbled in carrying the biggest and most delicious looking chocolate cake I'd ever seen. Lowering it upon a table in the centre of Room 6, she instructed us to describe it using as many of the five senses as possible; how it looked, smelled, tasted and what it felt like to touch. While the first four were easy, the fifth sense proved a little trickier,

"Red light! Red light!" Sebastian groaned as he stumbled upon this conundrum.

"What is it, Sebastian?" Mrs Murphy asked, forcing her eyes from the gleaming, brown icing.

"How can I describe what a cake sounds like when it doesn't talk?" the confused boy asked.

"Ah well, maybe you could describe what it might say if it was alive?" Mrs Murphy suggested. Though the patient teacher was trying to be helpful, Sebastian was incapable of imagining anything.

"Don't be ridiculous Miss! Cakes can't talk," the confused boy replied in a matter of fact tone while we struggled to suppress the giggles lurking in our throats, "and I'm glad they don't talk because I would feel very mean about eating them if they did."

"Okay. Well, I suppose that's true," Mrs Murphy patiently countered, "so, why don't we describe the words we might say when we see the cake or after we sample a slice?"

"YUM!" Sebastian instantly replied before quickly jotting down his three chosen letters and dramatically stamping them with an exclamation mark.

"Can we eat it now?" he bluntly asked as we finally surrendered to the swell of giggles and fell about laughing.

"It's really just for show Sebastian. How will the year five students describe it after lunch if we've devoured it?" the exasperated teacher reasoned.

"We could take a picture of it before we eat it!" Sebastian suggested with a look of deadly seriousness.

Mrs Mayhew's morning assembly had certainly stirred the appetites of everyone at Thrive Academy. Before lunch, our third workshop was hosted by a local poet, Marjorie

Miller, who popped by to read us some of her 'funny' poems. We should have filled the classroom with laughter when she told us *The Tale of The Sky Diving Walrus,* but Jarvis and Simon wouldn't allow it. Sneering and sniping, they eye-balled anyone who even slightly tittered. Because they had decided that 'funny' poems should only amuse the "babies" in Year 1, we all sat quietly and kept our joy to ourselves. I felt terrible for Marjorie and hoped that all the younger year groups gave her the giggles her hilarious poems deserved.

After trying and failing to make us laugh with one final poem, Marjorie gave up and instead offered us some tips and advice about how to create quirky, silly rhymes. Handing out fresh sheets of lined paper, she invited us to write our own poems about "any place, person or object you wish."

"I can't think of anything!" Jarvis' declared before lifting his pen.

"Think of something you feel passionate

about. Something or someone you can't live without," a deflated Marjorie offered patiently.

"Oh! Oh! I know," Jarvis rambled while hurriedly scribbling, "I'll write about the imminent return of Blafferty The Legend!"

Instead of writing a poem, I sneakily scribbled the speech that would fill my two minutes at that evening's meeting in the village hall. With time running out, I had to try and write something. I had to find the right words to capture a most incredible week; the words that would convince the governors to make the correct decision and ensure we hadn't witnessed our last ever Mrs Mayhew morning assembly.

"Can I borrow your stapler?" I whispered to A.J. who was generally better stocked than W.H. Smith.

"Paper clip or stapler. Whichever you prefer?" she offered.

Plumping for the latter, I accepted the mini, green stapler that looked like a sharp-toothed frog. After clipping my three pages together, I placed them proudly on my desk as if I had finally finished the first draft of my masterpiece, *Searching for Starlight.*

Marjorie noticed that I'd finished, "You there. Sorry, I don't know your name: the girl with the lovely red hair. Would you mind sharing a few lines with us?" she asked.

Though I would have loved for Jarvis and his cronies to hear every word I'd written about Mrs Mayhew, none of my lines rhymed. Frantically, I tried to make something up on the spot but my tongue was clicking, my lips were sticking, and I couldn't think of anything. Much to my surprise, Jarvis intervened for me,

"Miss, Willow is a selective mute. She only talks if it rains on a bank holiday."

For the last few days, A.J. had blocked my every attempt at retaliation, but this time she didn't have a chance. Without thinking, I grabbed the frog stapler and flung it across the room quicker than a cowboy could draw his pistol in a shoot-out at the Ok Corral. The mini-stationery soared through the air until it smashed Jarvis right in the mouth. Dark, red blood spurted from his top lip.

"OWWWWWW!" he screamed in exaggerated agony, holding his face like his jaw was hanging loose. "Miss, did you see that?"

"Willow Hushley! Get out of this room this instant!" Mrs Murphy screamed without really knowing why.

Within ten minutes of being called, dad arrived to meet Mrs Mayhew. As she welcomed him into her office with an open hand, dad wiped his greasy paw in his overalls and blushed. I kept my gaze firmly on the worn, linoleum floor. The last thing I needed to see was that all too familiar look in his eyes – that sorrowful mix of hurt and disappointment saddled by a ruffled, scornful brow that said, "haven't we been through enough?"

I had been in that position and witnessed that hang-dog look enough times to know better but so long as there were Jarvis Bonsons in the world, I knew that I would never be far from a seat outside a head teacher's office.

Craning my neck towards the door, I tried and failed to overhear the likely judgements. It was a short conversation, and after their brief deliberation, dad walked out to deliver the verdict,

"You! Home! Now!" he ordered. "What do you have to say to Mrs Mayhew?"

"I'm really sorry Miss," I offered without raising my eyes from the floor.

"You're grounded for a week. No phone. No iPad. Nothing!" dad snapped.

I could have fought back and argued that, "it was about time someone stapled that bully's lips shut". I could have thrown a tantrum and revealed every hurtful word and spiteful comment that Jarvis had spluttered about me, A.J. and anyone else who dared walk within his line of vision but I knew it wouldn't wash. The blood I drew was red and running and visible. The hurt he caused EVERY SINGLE DAY was not.

Before we left, dad turned back to Mrs Mayhew to ask if she could, "please pass on my apologies to the boy and let his parents know how sorry we are. I'm happy to speak to them myself if you think it'd help."

"No problem," Mrs Mayhew replied with a little tap of her right hand on her folded left arm.

As I followed my stomping father through the school gate, I took my speech from my blazer pocket, crumpled it up and tossed it in the bin.

20

'The Girl with the Zipped-Up Lips'

"You're lucky Mrs Mayhew is so understanding," dad warned as we trudged through the door of STINKIN' SCREAMIN' RUBBISH HOLE. "If she wasn't, we could well be looking for yet another new school," he raged as he flung his keys onto the kitchen counter.

"And I'll likely need a new job if I keep having to leave halfway through the day!" he barked before slapping his jacket onto the kitchen table.

There was nothing to be said. No reply could fix this mess. So I didn't.

"Phone! Now!" he demanded with an outstretched palm before snapping it from me.

"Go change out of your uniform and don't dare leave that room 'til I call you for dinner," he ordered.

As I moved to climb the stair, that hippo-filled suitcase was heavier than ever before. Tears welled within my eyes as I struggled to heave my lead-filled legs up each step. Everything was crumbling, everything was collapsing and I was the one swinging the wrecking ball. I had spoiled my last day with Mrs Mayhew, destroyed dad's day at work and damaged any chance I had of attending the meeting in the village hall.

The age of Mayhew would soon be over. Blafferty was ready to make his comeback, and I was powerless to stop it. Changing into my emoji pyjamas (one of which perfectly summed up my mood. Yes! The brown one!), I pulled the curtains shut and climbed under my duvet. I needed mum's lullaby more than ever before. I needed to hear her voice and feel her near.

The instant I wrapped my headphones around my head, her angelic voice fell from the heavens, filled my ears and inflated my heart.

"...know that I'm not far..."

"...I'm in between those stars..."

She was so loud and so clear. It felt like she was snuggling into me. Just like she did when I was little: lying on the cold side of the quilt with her long, red hair spilling across the pillow we shared while her right arm draped across my stomach like a seat belt.

"...I'll be with you day and night..."

"...I'm in between starlight."

That evening, the simple rhymes and reassuring words rolled around my head, and in the darkening room, I sang along. I was no longer afraid that some other song or long-winded conversation might take mum from me; her lullaby had been downloaded into my head and heart forever. Like Mother & Daughter Hushley live in concert, we sang as one until my tired eyes and worn out body insisted it was time for sleep.

When dad rushed through my bedroom door sometime later, I mistakenly thought he was calling me for dinner until I noticed he was clutching the keys of his rust bucket van in his right hand.

"I've got to go," he announced without checking if I was awake, "I've had five calls in ten minutes from locals who've had their tyres deflated, so I better go and make up for the half day's pay I lost. There's some pizza on the side."

Blinking my sleepy eyes awake, I fumbled around my bedside cabinet for my phone until the memory of dad's demanding palm reappeared. Thankfully, my alarm clock was happy to tell me it was seventeen minutes past six.

"Evening news!" I thought as I quickly rolled my duvet away and snatched my dressing gown from the back of my bedroom door. Slinging it over my shoulder, I moved to break free of my carpeted prison, but as I swung the door back, a loud thud on my bedroom window made me jump higher than heaven.

Though I had no idea what it was, it was loud enough to scatter dragons. Frozen, I tilted my head to the right (the way dogs do when confused by their master's instruction). Fearing I might have imagined it, I waited a moment to see if it came knocking once more.

A second thud arrived, louder than the first which was instantly followed by a third whack, louder than them all. It was so thunderous; it dried my throat, and fluttered my heart. Something or someone was knocking at my bedroom window, and I was utterly alone in the house.

"Maybe it's a little bird," I optimistically hoped, "or maybe a massive giant has caught the scent of my pizza and wants to eat it before gobbling me up for dessert!" I fretted as my imagination ran wild.

Slowly and breathlessly, I tip-toed towards the left side of the curtain and gingerly nudged the drape back with my nose in an attempt to spy my uninvited guest.

"Oh thank god!" I sighed, finally catching my breath.

It was a bird. An A.J. shaped bird flapping her arms about while hopping on one shoe in my front garden.

"Willow! Willow! Quick, let me in!" she shouted hoarsely through a cupped hand the instant she spotted me.

"What are you doing and why are you wearing one shoe?" I shouted after flicking back the curtain and pushing the window open.

"I couldn't find any small stones, so my shoe was all I had! Now let me in!" she squealed while squirming about like she was seconds from wetting her pants.

"You can't come in! I'm grounded, and dad could be back any second," I announced in a stern, grown-up voice.

"Not likely!" A.J. spurted with a knowing smile.

"What do you mean - not likely?"

"Well, I've spent the last hour adjusting the tyre pressure of ten different automobiles located in every corner of this village which means forty tyres are now in need of your father's assistance. Master Hushley shall not be returning to the residence for quite some time," she revealed in a weird, posh voice while holding a slightly bent pen-knife aloft in her right hand.

"Now let me in!" the tire stabber demanded.

While I did invite her in, it wasn't an invitation to eat anything and everything she desired. The instant she spotted my half-moon pizza on the sideboard, she seized it, chewed it and swallowed it without even asking.

"I'm starving," she said with her mouth half-full of melted cheese and warmed bread, "stabbing car tyres isn't like popping balloons you know."

I was still in a daze. Three minutes earlier I was sound asleep but now dad was gone, and the pizza-stealing-tire-stabber was blabbing away in my kitchen,

"If we watch the news here and leave right away, we should be at the village hall for seven," she mumbled as I filled a glass with cold water from the sink.

"Oh you are too kind," she exclaimed after nabbing the glass from my hand before I could even lift it towards my mouth.

By the time I poured the second glass of water, A.J. had vacated the kitchen with the last slice of *my* pizza and was now standing in *my* sitting room pointing the remote control at *my* TV.

"I do hope the assembly made it!" she gushed while perched on the edge of the coffee table, literally inches from the large, flat screen.

As the drum-laden intro to the Evening News began, I flounced into the armchair behind her.

"Bradley's telling everyone you've been expelled," she revealed while glancing over her shoulder to check if this nonsense was somehow true.

I shook my head and bit my bottom lip which spoke louder than any words could.

"While I think your PJ's are absolutes adorables, I would advise you get dressed. No one's going to take us seriously if you've got poop emojis smeared across your back," she rambled while chewing.

As I stood up to go and get changed, the newsreader's opening words made my lashes launch from my eyelids.

"Good evening. Our main story starts in the little village of Ickleton where today, we met one extraordinary young girl who has, with the help of her head-teacher, found her voice after three years of silence."

"YESSSS!" A.J. wailed before vaulting towards me like a flying starfish which sent me reeling backwards and pinned me to the sofa cushions.

"We did it! We did it!" she wailed like she'd scored the winning goal in the dying seconds of a World Cup final.

The next three minutes were a blur. I dedicated the first ten seconds to shushing A.J. up while pushing the 'volume +' down as hard as I could until I finally realised I was holding the remote control the wrong way round. From what we did manage to eventually see (and hear), the story covered not only Friday morning's assembly but also captured much of the Mayhew mayhem that had descended on Thrive Academy over the last five days. Along with the (utterly cringe) interview with myself, they asked Mrs Murphy how she felt about Mr Blafferty's possible return,

"It's not my place to say," she gushed while blushing into the camera, "however I was very close to abandoning teaching before Mrs Mayhew arrived. But these past few days have been so strange and so marvellous, I think she's helped me fall back in love with it all over again."

There was also a phone conversation with Ms Gibby, my Year 5 teacher from school #3, who revealed that "during the eight months I worked with Willow, I tried everything I could think of to help her open up and speak to us yet nothing worked. Whatever Mrs Mayhew has done to help her find her voice must have been something special because I tried every trick in the book but her lips stayed zipped."

"C'mon, we've got to go. Please ditch the P.J.s!" A.J. insisted as Emily Nouveaux, who was reporting live from outside the village hall, wrapped up the news story with a reminder about the governor meeting.

It was almost five to seven by the time we whipped the front door behind us and raced down Cuckoo Hill. The dusky sky pulsed with a purpose and despite not knowing what else we could do to keep Mrs Mayhew in our lives, we had to ensure *Blah Blah* Blafferty never set foot on that assembly hall stage again.

21

A S.M.A.R.P. Discovery

"**Y**ou are very belated in your arrival," Sebastian scolded as we reached the village hall at one minute past seven.

Members of the sizeable crowd were blabbing about my interview on the evening news. "That's the girl who didn't talk," I heard one busy-body murmur while pointing me out to her friend. Thankfully, most of the locals were too interested in congregating around the news reporter in the hope of squeezing their cheesy grin on camera to bother with me.

"Willow, this is my father, Gerald," Sebastian revealed as a tall, smart-suited man stepped towards me and smiled, "dad, this is my friend, Willow."

"Nice to finally meet you Willow. Our chair of governors is definitely going to want to hear from you. Have you got your speech or a few notes about what you'd like to say?" he asked.

While it was a question I should have expected, his words instantly squeezed the air from my lungs as they recalled a most terrible thought; MY SPEECH WAS IN THE BIN!

Without reply, I spun on my heel and ran.

"Willow, where are you going?" A.J. called but I couldn't spare a second to stop and explain,

"I'm coming too!" she yelled and followed without knowing why.

"Red light! Red light!" Sebastian wailed as we ran from where we were needed.

"Where are you going?" A.J. asked when she finally caught up with me.

"When I left school with dad I threw my speech in the bin outside the gate," I explained through wheezy panting and the clomping of our galloping feet.

"But the caretaker's probably emptied the bins already," A.J. offered, trying to add a layer of common sense to the crazy cake I was baking.

"I know but I have to try. Everything that needs to be said is on that paper and I'll never be able to speak without it," I insisted.

As we arrived at the school, I was relieved to find the lights on and the gates open.

"Hopefully the caretaker hasn't got round to it yet," I blindly wished as I crouched to catch my breath.

"Was it this bin?" A.J. asked while I nodded my silent reply.

Tilting my head to the side, I stooped down to peer inside but the moment I looked, my thumping heart sank,

"Typical!" I shouted before kicking the bin in frustration.

Lined with a shining black, plastic bag; the bin was empty. My speech was gone. My words were lost.

"I know you're not far mum," I cried with

my head tilted skyward, not caring that A.J. was listening, "but whatever stars you're in between tonight, please help me fix this. Help me save Mrs Mayhew," I begged before kicking the bin once more.

Though I never requested my feet to do so, they instantly marched inside the school gate. While my brain was scrambling to figure out what I was doing, the rest of my body seemed to know exactly what needed to be done.

"The old bag might still be in there," I proposed after noticing that a wedge of chipped wood was holding the assembly hall door open.

Before tip-toeing in, we slowly craned our necks around the doorway to double-triple check no-one was inside but despite our best attempts to be as light-footed as super spy ninjas, we were as quiet as a troop of baby elephants playing hop-scotch.

Thankfully, the coast was clear but when we entered the hall, there was no sign of the tied-up bin-bag.

"Surely, you can remember at least some of the speech," A.J. implored as all hope and time finally ran out.

But before I could answer, a loud body-less voice suddenly filled the hall,

"What do you mean I'm late?" the slightly muffled and very irritated voice demanded from behind the stage curtains.

A.J. got such a fright that she had to put her hand over her own mouth to stop herself from screaming.

"Who is that?" I mouthed theatrically without sound.

Although the voice was familiar, I couldn't place it. Twitching my head, I searched for somewhere to hide. We were too far from the entrance to make it back, and as all the chairs had been stacked away, we couldn't hide behind them. Like statues, we stood frozen in the centre of the hall. We were moments from being found out - seconds from being spotted. I wished my feet would assume control like they did before because my brain was faltering like a stuck record.

"They can wait for me - it pays to be fashionably late," the voice came again, louder than before and now clear enough for me to place it.

"BLAFFERTY!" I mouthed towards A.J. through bulging eyes.

Mr *Blah! Blah!* was back. It had been a week since I heard his smug, scratchy tone and now it sounded more pompous than ever. Without warning, A.J. tip-toed *TOWARDS* the stage. Without asking them to do so, my feet followed.

"What are you doing? That's where he is!" I delicately whispered but my naughty, stubborn feet and my weird, crazy friend were both refusing to listen.

After reluctantly reaching the stage, I winced and braced myself for impact because I was sure that he was seconds from pulling back that blue curtain. His voice was so loud; I could almost smell what he had for dinner,

"I'm just at the school now. I had to check-in to make sure that circus act hadn't trashed my office. I want everything ship-shape for my return on Monday."

Lifting my arms into the air and shaking my open hands, I mimed to A.J., "What are you doing?" She didn't respond but pointed towards a small brown latch fixed to one of the wooden panels at the front of the stage. Without even considering if there might be enough space for two human bodies amongst all the old gym equipment and broken chairs, A.J. crouched down, quietly lifted the latch, swung back the wooden panel on its hinge and dived in. With no alternative, I followed.

Tingles of panic shuddered down my spine as a strange smell of plastic and dust infiltrated my nose. Pawing around in the darkness, I tried to be super-ninja-spy quiet, but as I turned to pull the door shut, I brushed against something that gave me such a fright, it forced a tiny squeal from my lips which sounded like someone had pinched a mouse.

"SHUSH! And stay still!" A.J. whispered like a frustrated parent.

Just as I pulled the panel shut, a loud thunk gave me an almighty hop.

Thunk!

Thunk!

Thunk!

Blafferty was coming down the stairs; plonking his feet heavily upon each step. I held my breath and prayed that he hadn't heard my squeak nor spotted the panel closing. My very sensible father never let me watch horror movies, but at that moment, I felt like I was actually in one; *Attack of the Pompous Principal.*

"I hope this pathetic little news story isn't going to affect the vote," he warned. His voice was muffled but still loud enough to be heard. While I had no idea whom he was talking to, they were clearly doing most of the yapping as long silences drifted between his every BLAH!

Neither A.J. nor I moved a muscle. I didn't dare breathe for fear my inflating and deflating stomach might knock against whatever had rustled. It was so dark beneath the stage, I couldn't tell the difference between my eyes being open or shut and while A.J. must have been less than a foot away from me, I couldn't see her at all.

"I know I've only got five minutes to state my case, but I doubt I'll need to say much at all as you've assured me this vote is a done deal, and I expect you to keep your word," he rasped.

The moment his words were in my ears, I cracked my neck towards where I assumed A.J.'s head would be. My eyes were ablaze with the hope that she'd heard exactly what I'd heard. This was a conspiracy that Bradley Bogstein would die to hear about. Questions raced around my mind; who was he talking to? Had the vote already been rigged?

"Anyway, let Mrs Deehan know, I'm on my way," he added as his voice faded.

Finally, his departing footsteps grew quieter and quieter until they disappeared. Even my ears breathed a sigh of relief as I exhaled and relaxed. Well, I was relaxed until A.J.'s face suddenly lit up and triggered a proper throat-scraper of a scream to rocket from my mouth.

"It's me," she said with a mischievous smile lit with the torch on her mobile phone.

"Bin bags!" I squeaked in a revelatory whisper, "We're sitting on bin bags!"

I couldn't quite believe my eyes; we had somehow stumbled upon the one thing that we were searching for.

"Thanks, mum!" I wheezed before blowing out a balloon sized sigh of relief.

Popping open the panel, I crawled out and checked that the coast was clear. Thankfully, Blafferty wasn't silently waiting in the hall to *SURPRISE!* us.

"Hopefully these are the bags they changed tonight," I prayed while A.J. crawled out behind me, dragging a bag in her right hand.

"But why is the caretaker storing everyone's crumby crisp packets and uneaten sandwich crusts under the stage?" she wondered while I attempted to untie the small, tight knot before giving up and ripping the plastic with my nails.

"What's in there?" she asked.

"Just paper," I replied before dumping my hand in and clawing out a handful, "just strips of shredded paper."

"How big was your speech?" A.J. quipped as she ripped hers open to reveal the exact same thing: shredded paper.

As I dropped my bag in exasperation, one thin strip of paper flicked up into the air and twirled around before landing by my feet. Picking it up, my eye was drawn to one particular word, scratched in faint, grey pencil.

"Zurich," I said as my forehead creased with a curious wrinkle.

"Don't you mean Geneva?" A.J. instinctively replied.

Grabbing the black bag at my feet, I turned it upside down and spilt its contents out on to the hard, varnished floor.

"Look!" I said to A.J. holding the strip of paper towards her, "This isn't all typed; someone's written 'Zurich' in pencil."

Snatching the paper from my fingers, A.J. studied it intently while I plucked another from the pile and read it aloud, "What is the square root of eighty-one?"

"NINE!" she shouted like a crazed contestant on a TV game show, desperate to win millions.

"These are SMARP tests!" I yelped.

A.J.'s eyes lit up as if she'd remembered the precise location of a doughnut she'd forgotten to eat. But, as quickly as they'd lit up, they soon faded,

"But why have they been shredded?" she wondered, "Wasn't that why Seb's dad was annoyed - because he wanted to see where Seb had gone wrong in his exams, but Blafferty wouldn't show him."

"I think so. But why is he shredding them and how come none of them have been marked?" I replied before dropping a random handful to the floor like the world's most boring confetti.

"If the SMARP machine is state of the art then it probably just reads the answer and totals up the score, it doesn't tick it or make comments like teachers do," A.J. speculated, trying to make sense of it all.

"But why do all the tests have to be shredded? Why wouldn't he file them or just throw them away? Why cut up them all up and hide them under the stage?" I pondered.

My curiosity was growing into frustration; each question was giving birth to at least three more big, fat baby questions.

"Explain the meaning of the word "revelation"?" A.J. asked in her best quiz show host voice after inspecting another sliver of paper.

"I know!" I yelped.

A thought suddenly struck me; not a full, perfectly coloured in thought but it was almost there,

"Maybe..." I said while wandering towards the pit of doom. Craning my arm inside, I plucked out as many black bags as possible in order to create some space.

"Maybe what?" A.J. inquired.

"Follow me and bring your phone!" I yelled as I began crawling through the black cave on my hunkers.

Because the sports hall (or "study hall" as Blafferty rebranded it) connected to the back of the assembly hall, I suspected that the stage might be connected to the back of the SMARP machine.

Crawling behind me, A.J. held her phone aloft to light our way, but the further we tunnelled, the harder it was to find space; bag after bag after bag blocked us like a black-plastic army.

"There must be a trillion tests papers in here!" A.J. surmised.

With little air around me, I held myself up with one arm while trying to shove bags from my path. My forehead streamed with sweat, my chest wheezed with dust but after fifty years of digging and sifting and wriggling and moving; I discovered the treasure I craved.

"There!" I said, pointing towards the end of the cave. A.J. lifted her phone higher, shining her torch towards it.

A letterbox of light.

"We're inside the SMARP machine!" I announced in a tight, raspy breath.

The under-stage gradually narrowed at each side but grew higher from the floor; *as tall as a wheelie bin and as wide a garage door.*

While I couldn't quite stand up, it was considerably easier to move about. The air was cooler. The light was brighter. Shuffling towards the jagged mouth of the SMARP machine, I felt like a dentist inspecting a shark's teeth. I anticipated seeing all sorts of different coloured wires and little mechanical boxes that looked fragile and expensive but all I saw was two sharp, shining pipes with jagged interlocking edges connected by dusty but dainty cogs. Just below the letterbox sat a large, black, open-mouthed bin bag half-full of grated exam papers.

"It looks like an office paper shredder," I said as I peered through the gap into the empty sports hall beyond. A.J. shone her light over my shoulder as I continued to ramble, "but surely it connects to the wifi to transfer the test scores to the ticket printing machine. Otherwise, how would he know the order for the ranking assembly?"

"Willow, look!" A.J. yelped after pointing her torch into the corner of the large box we were standing in. "There's a plug socket here. It's switched off, and the wire's running through a hole in the wall. There's one on the other side too. Maybe the scores are sent through these?"

"But they look just like normal plugs, I doubt they transfer information," I bit back.

"What about this little box?" A.J. offered as she knelt down by the plug.

"Let me see!" I asked.

Nudging her slightly, I snatched her phone and shone the light towards her discovery. Despite being only slightly bigger than a matchbox, tiny, raised letters were moulded into the green plastic.

"It's a list with six options," I announced in a thick whisper before reading them aloud,

"One. Combination.

Two. In waves

Three. Slo Glo (their spelling, not mine!)

Four. Flashing

Five. Slow Fade

Six. Christmas Twinkle."

"Are you winding me up?" A.J. asked while nudging me slightly in order to get a closer look.

"No, I'm not. That's exactly what it says. These are Christmas tree lights!"

The words of my speech might have been lost to the local rubbish dump but in that very moment I knew I'd discovered the key that could lock Blafferty out of Thrive Academy for good.

"But he said the flashing wires were the brain of the SMARP machine. He said the flashing showed the machine was thinking as it marked our exams," A.J. recalled.

"That's exactly what he said - a million pound cutting-edge technology - but it's nothing more than Christmas tree lights shoved inside a plastic tube taped to a paper shredder," I replied.

"What shall we do because if we don't get back soon, the meeting will be over?" A.J. asked.

"We need to drop these bags in front of Blafferty and demand that he explains it!"

"Shouldn't we bring the light with us too?"

"I'll grab the bags if you bring the lights!" I directed as a shudder of anticipation circled my soul.

"Eh, the plug's too big to fit through the hole," A.J. moaned before she suddenly thought of a solution, "but if I use my knife to undo the plug, then you can pull the wire through before I reattach it on the other side."

In less than sixty seconds, the pen-knife expert had detached the plug and followed me from the pit of doom. Streams of sweat dripped down her face and neck but her smile was wider than the mouth of the SMARP machine.

"Let's wipe the smugness from that clown's face," A.J. declared as we ran through the sports hall with a black bag in each hand and the coiled string of Christmas lights wrapped around my shoulder.

"Give me your phone a sec!" I panted.

"What for?" A.J. asked.

"I want to see how much a paper shredder costs on Amazon?"

22

Shining Lights

Whizzing past the waiting crowd, we crashed through the swinging, glass panelled doors and flopped our black, plastic plunder upon the floor like a couple of swashbuckling pirates.

While we gasped for breath, a sea of staggered faces, sitting around a large, rectangular table, spun in our direction. Blafferty who was plonked at the far, right corner of the table had to blink to stop his eyes from exploding from his skull the instant he spotted our bin bag booty. It was in that very moment that I knew. I knew we had definitely dug up something he didn't want the world to see: something he hoped would stay buried.

"Sorry, we're late!" A.J. bellowed before

resting her hands on her knees as if she had just run the London marathon.

"Excuse me!" Mrs Bonson fumed through a furious face that was redder than a stack of dynamite, "I was speaking!"

"You're excused!" A.J. replied cheekily, almost setting the fuse alight.

"I'm sorry Mrs Deehan," Sebastian's father gushed towards the chair of governors who was seated at the head of the table, "this is A.J. and Willow. They are the girls I invited along to represent the views of the students."

Mrs Deehan was an elderly lady with a kind smile and soft, white hair which made her look a lot like Mrs Claus.

"Thank you, Gerald. Children, I'm sorry to say that you were scheduled to speak at five past seven. I'm afraid it wouldn't be appropriate for you to be here for the rest of the meeting. Sebastian has already had his say and was just about to leave," she patiently explained.

"Here! Here!" Blafferty bellowed without

adjusting his gaze from our loot.

"We'll be super quick Mrs Deehan," A.J. immediately responded, "and we've got something you definitely need to see."

The white-haired lady thought for a second while glancing around the table, measuring the likely reaction to such a move.

"Well okay, let's give Mrs Bonson a moment to finish her point, and then you can have your say," she suggested with a gentle nod.

"But I've just started speaking!" Mrs Bonson raged through her raspberry face.

"Please be prompt," Mrs Deehan advised, "we have heard quite a lot from you lately."

"OOH! BURN!" I thought while strangling a giggle.

Clearing her throat, Mrs Bonson returned to her moaning and groaning about the need for "academic excellence" and for her son to be "pushed to the very limit of his mental agility."

"My son hasn't sat an exam in almost seven

days!" she fumed via spitting lips and a frothing mouth. "It's just not normal!"

"YOU'RE NOT NORMAL!" A.J. suddenly barked, drawing gasps from the table while Mrs Bonson's fruit-bomb face swelled to the brink of explosion. But before anyone could scold or interrupt, A.J. was determined to finish her point.

"There is no such thing as normal, everyone's normal is different," she bellowed before winking towards Sebastian who was sat by his father's side, "Mrs Mayhew is the most amazing person I've ever met, and I hope she doesn't stay for just a few more weeks or a few more years - "

"Can somebody PLEASE shut her up!" Mrs Bonson thundered as she slammed her hand upon the desk.

A monsoon mixed with a hurricane could not have shut A.J. up. She was on a roll. All of the times she was too afraid to act now amassed into one mega, giant ball of super ACTION!

"Every night this week, I've prayed that she will stay at our school long enough to not only teach me but to teach my children and my grandchildren because if they get to see one-tenth of what I got to see or feel one-fifth of what I got to feel, then I know they will experience something that most people never, ever do."

Every word flowing from A.J.'s mouth was faultlessly delivered. We never found my speech, but at that very moment, she found all the right words to say,

"We may not have been pushed to the very limit of our academic agility but Mrs Mayhew has taught us things that no never- ending SMARP exam ever could."

"Like what?" Mrs Bonson snapped with an accusing glare that was so sharp and so direct; it startled A.J. and briefly tied her tongue in a knot.

"Tell us what you've learned?" she barked again, cementing A.J.'s silence.

In that silence, I stepped forward. I might have lost my speech, but the last four lines were perched on the tip of my tongue,

"We learned to live our lives to the full and never find them dull. We learned that we will soar to greater heights if we crawl, then walk, then fly. We learned that if we wait for the right moment to arrive, in that moment, we will thrive. We learned that if we don't give up and don't give in, if we stay the course, we will win."

I fell silent.

Nobody reacted.

No smiles. No grimaces.

No claps. No boos.

Everyone stared.

"And we will win!" A.J. suddenly chirped as she waltzed towards the rectangular table holding a black bag aloft. Before the gaze of the silent spectators, she lifted it towards the table and tipped the contents out.

"What is this?" Mrs Bonson squealed as she snapped up strips of shredded paper between her fingers and inspected it with bulging eyes.

"Mrs Bonson, I'm sure if you gave your mouth a rest and your ears a chance, the girls might begin to explain," Mrs Deehan decreed in a calm but assertive tone, "and may I remind everyone, including our young guests, that this is a formal meeting and we must all behave in a cordial manner and should refrain from interrupting or shouting over one another. A.J., please tell us about the contents of your bag."

"Ehm, we've only brought over two bags but there are at least two hundred like these stuffed under the assembly hall stage that are all full of shredded SMARP ex-"

"Absolute poppycock!" Blafferty spat.

"Excuse me Mr Blafferty, I've just said we will have no interruptions. If you do that again, I must insist you leave," Mrs Deehan reminded with a touch of impatience.

"I do apologise Chair, but you must understand that one hundred and eighteen exams were scanned into my SMARP machine every day and marked using my cutting-edge technology. The reason they are shredded is that I simply had no way of storing them," Blafferty bluffed in a far from convincing tone.

"Your cutting-edge technology is the greatest hoax in history. Your SMARP machine is a bog-standard office paper shredder which anyone can buy for thirty pounds on Amazon!" I snapped back with a straight face while everyone around me sat a little higher in their chairs.

This was getting interesting.

"Absolute balderdash!" Blafferty spat, "My SMARP education programme cost one point eight million pounds, and I have all the invoices to prove it. I will not have some girl walk in here and start spouting absolute pish-posh! You, young lady, have far too much to say for yourself!" he screamed, pointing a shaking finger towards me.

I didn't reply. I couldn't. I was too busy laughing at the idea that I, who hadn't spoken for almost three years, was being accused by BLAH BLAH BLAFFERTY of having too much to say.

"Well, Mr Blafferty, why don't you explain it to everyone," Mrs Deehan patiently requested.

"Well I... well... I ... it's the future of education. It's state of the art technology," he blathered unconvincingly.

"I didn't ask you to describe it Mr Blafferty. I've asked you to simply explain how it works. The girls are saying that the machine looks strikingly similar to an office shredder and they've found many bags of shredded paper. Now, can you put the girls straight by telling us all how it works?" Mrs Deehan (im)patiently requested.

"Well, it might look simple, but it's very, very complex. Once I scan the exam paper, the machine automatically marks the questions and sends signals through high-tech wiring to my SMARP computer which then ranks all the students in order of their results. I then use that informa-"

"You're lying!" A.J. flared.

"She interrupted me!" Mr Blafferty cried like a cranky, spoiled child.

"A.J., please let Mr Blafferty finish," the Chair ordered with a thinly disguised grin.

"We use the information to rank everyone in our morning assembly," he trailed off, still sulking about being interrupted.

"We found those *high-tech* wires you're referring to," I announced before unrolling them from my shoulder and passing them to the governor closest to me, "please take a look and pass them along. I would particularly like to draw your attention to the small green box near the plug."

My heart was beating so fast; I feared the drumming might drown out the sound coming from my lips. Grabbing hold of the lights, Sebastian's dad inspected the little, green box for a moment before suddenly turning his head towards the now blushing Blafferty,

"Mr Blafferty, can you explain what these lights actually do?" he calmly asked.

"Ehmm – eh –," Blafferty groaned while twisting uncomfortably in his chair.

"Mr Blafferty, they are not words. They are just sounds. Are these lights part of your SMARP machine and what do they do?" Mr Topple pushed.

"Ehmmm – eh -," Blafferty groaned while twisting some more.

"I'll do it!" A.J. interjected, scooping the lights from his hands before heading towards a plug socket that she'd spotted on the back wall of the hall.

Blafferty suddenly stood up.

"Don't plug them in!" he bawled.

"Why?" I asked.

"Because - because - they need to be connected to the school system to work. Otherwise, they're just - just -," his voice fading to silence.

"They're just what?" I asked again while stretching my hand towards the light switch near the entrance, poised to switch it off.

Nobody needed to answer because in that very moment, A.J. plugged the lights in just as I flicked the hall lights off.

"Red light! Red light!" Sebastian screamed the instant the fairy lights lit up the corner of the hall.

"Yellow light! Yellow light!

Green light! Green light!

Blue light! Blue light!" he chanted while A.J. clicked through the buttons.

"This one's Christmas Twinkle," she announced, her face lit by an array of Christmassy colours.

While the flickering lights drew everyone's attention, Mr Blafferty slowly eased his chair back from the table and crept towards the exit. For a moment, I let him think he might escape undetected before I flicked the hall lights back on.

"Excuse me, Mr Blafferty, where are you off to?" Mrs Deehan asked.

"Ehmmm - ehm - I'm somewhat afraid of the dark," he pathetically lied.

"Mr Blafferty, if what these two young girls are saying is true, there will be some serious questions about what you did spend the money on because these Christmas lights are certainly not 'cutting edge' technology!" the chair of governors scolded.

"Eleven-nintey-nine on Amazon!" A.J. shouted while wrapping the string of lights back around her arm.

Stone-silent Blafferty gazed towards Mrs Bonson who was doing everything she could to avoid his stare. His face flushed red. His eyes bulged, and finally I realised who was on the other end of that phone,

"You said this vote was sorted!" he erupted while pointing a crooked finger towards the startled woman. Instinctively, she leaned to her right in a feeble attempt to depart the zone of blame.

"You promised me it was a done deal!" he continued to rage, "You told me that imbecile Mrs Mayhew would not even last a week, that you had picked her because her best friend was a meerkat. You said she could not even talk properly. You said she had a stutter!"

"Mr Blafferty, please sit down so we can discuss this sensibly," Mrs Deehan proclaimed in an attempt to restore order.

But Mr Blafferty didn't sit down.

He ran.

He ran fast.

Through the door.

Past the crowd.

Past Cuckoo Hill.

Past Thrive Academy and out of our lives forever.

"Well, girls. I must say I'm glad you arrived when you did," Mrs Deehan declared, "I will have to investigate these claims fully and I'm particularly curious about how Mr Blafferty thought tonight's vote was a done deal and why he was so sure Mrs Mayhew would not last a week," she added while staring directly towards Mrs Bonson who was suddenly fascinated with the floor.

"What about Monday?" I impatiently blurted.

"On Monday, Mrs Mayhew will take morning assembly and on Tuesday and on Wednesday and for however long she wishes," Mrs Deehan beamed.

Vaulting towards me, A.J. sprang into my arms and screamed,

"We did it! She's staying!"

I didn't know what to say.

I was utterly gobsmacked.

I was completely speechless.

Epilogue

The day after the governor meeting, Mr Blafferty was arrested at London City Airport trying to board a private jet to the South of France. The invoices he promised never materialised and the governors eventually discovered how "cutting edge" his SMARP machine truly was.

About a week later, a local evening news story revealed everything: Mr Blafferty built the SMARP machine using odd bits and bobs from his garage with one or two essential purchases from his Amazon Prime account. I also finally discovered how he managed to sync the flashing lights with the paper shredder as Emily Nouveaux revealed that he splashed a whopping £14.99 on a set of super-swanky remote-control fairy lights. With the remote control hidden in his pocket, he pressed it every time we fed our exams into the mouth of the shredder to make it look like the machine was "thinking".

The local evening news team also *exclusively* revealed that Mr Blafferty squandered the £1.8 million government investment on a flash BMW M5, some super swanky walking canes and a mahoosive mansion in Monaco with two swimming pools (indoor and outdoor!) as well as his own private jet which he used to travel back and forth to Ickleton every weekend.

Emily's sensational scoop also disclosed how Mrs Bonson had blindly supported Mr Blafferty for years: never questioning anything he did while doing everything she could to influence the governor's vote. Bradley Bogstein told anyone who would listen that he overheard Felicity Bonson trying to bribe three different governors with our record-breaking cake in an attempt to convince them to change their mind about Blafferty.

He also swore blind that, "The morning after the meeting in the village hall, I saw Jarvis and his mum sneak out their front door at three am. With the car packed, they drove down the road with no lights on to make sure no one spotted them."

What Bradley was doing up at 3am was a mystery in itself, but everyone enjoyed the story too much to bother questioning him. He also told everyone with a pair of ears that, "Jarvis was sent to an all-boys boarding school in Wales where he was pushed to the very limit of his academic agility."

Dad managed to fix all the tyres that were *mysteriously* deflated that Friday evening and recouped the money he lost from leaving the garage early to collect me from school. For his 40th birthday, I bought him a new kitchen radio with strict rules on which stations he was allowed listen to. No old man head-banger stuff - pop and r'n'b only.

With Jarvis gone and her confidence repaired, A.J. insisted everyone call her by the name on her birth certificate; Anodiwa, while she and her parents plan to travel to Zimbabwe next

Christmas to visit her grandmother.

At least once a week, Mum's lullaby still pops by to say hi, but now it has to share my brain with a new song; a seven beat, four-line song that I will never forget.

Monday's assembly was eye-poppingly, jaw-droppingly amazing. So too was the one after that and the one after that. In one of her assemblies, Mrs Mayhew told us all about her stutter; how it arrived one day when she was ten and how she didn't talk for many years after until her music teacher helped her use rhyme and rhythm to overcome it. She also showed us how easy it was to train a meerkat. (Believe me, it really is!) The talented family of six; Mr and Mrs Paradisi and the four mini-Paradisis were regularly spotted around Thrive Academy; playing their part in running the school.

Shortly after being appointed the "full-time" principal of Thrive Academy, Mrs Mayhew renamed the school, St. John's Primary, after St. John Chrysostom, the patron saint of public speakers. She also secured a one-million-pound government investment to transform every classroom into a fully accessible space for all children. She also organised specialist training to ensure all our teachers could support students with speech and language difficulties. (Don't worry! Every penny was accounted for!)

Eventually, the time came for Sebastian, Anodiwa, myself and everyone else in Year 6 to say goodbye to Mrs Mayhew, Mrs Murphy, Miss Patton, the Paradisis and all the staff at St. John's. Although we were sad to say goodbye (leavers day was a sob-fest!), we were super-duper excited about starting "big" school and we spent all summer wondering what the assemblies of our new head-teacher, Mr Pompisic, might be like.

But we knew that no matter what he said or what he did, it would never, ever match the magic and mayhem of a Mrs Mayhew morning assembly.

OTHER TITLES FROM JOHN CALLAGHAN

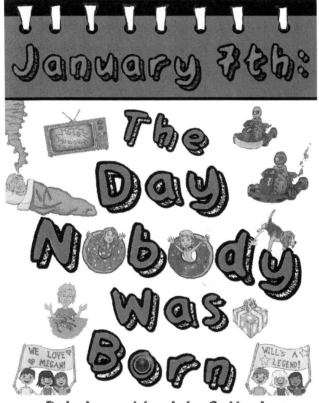

Debut novel by John Callaghan
with illustrations by Lisa Callaghan

Will Stills is the most ordinary boy in the world.

Trouble is, the whole world is convinced he's far from ordinary. Every January 7th, Will is forced to celebrate his birthday in the most peculiar way. But it is not his proud parents who are planning these bizarre parties! The twisted minds behind the world's biggest media company, ViewYou, are pulling the strings.

But what exactly are they are trying to prove?
What is it they want the world to see?
Why are they and everyone else so obsessed with Will Stills?

Available now via paperback and Kindle @ Amazon.co.uk

Printed in Great
Britain
by Amazon